"Lauren, about the other night..."

Rafe gave Lauren a rueful smile. "I'm sorry. I never intended to say what I did."

To his surprise, she smiled back. "That's okay. Forget about it," she said, almost cheerfully. "Actually, you did me a favor."

"I did?"

She nodded. "I thought over what you said, and I decided you were right."

That should have been a good thing, yet Rafe suddenly felt wary. As if he were in the marines again, picking his way through a field full of land mines. "Right about what?" he asked cautiously.

"What you're always telling me. That I need to develop some backbone. Set goals, get out more. That I should learn to fight for what I want."

Rafe relaxed again, leaning back in his chair. He gave her an approving nod, pleased that she was finally taking his advice. "Good. Glad to hear it. So what is it that you decided you want?"

"A man."

Dear Reader,

Celebrate the holidays with Silhouette Romance! We strive to deliver emotional, fast-paced stories that suit your every mood—each and every month. Why not give the gift of love this year by sending your best friends and family members one of our heartwarming books?

Sandra Paul's *The Makeover Takeover* is the latest page-turner in the popular HAVING THE BOSS'S BABY series. In Teresa Southwick's *If You Don't Know by Now,* the third in the DESTINY, TEXAS series, Maggie Benson is shocked when Jack Riley comes back into her life—and their child's!

I'm also excited to announce that this month marks the return of two cherished authors to Silhouette Romance. Gifted at weaving intensely dramatic stories, Laurey Bright once again thrills Romance readers with her VIRGIN BRIDES title, *Marrying Marcus.* Judith McWilliams's charming tale, *The Summer Proposal,* will delight her throngs of devoted fans and have us all yearning for more!

As a special treat, we have two fresh and original royalty-themed stories. In *The Marine & the Princess,* Cathie Linz pits a hardened military man against an impetuous princess. Nicole Burnham's *Going to the Castle* tells of a duty-bound prince who escapes his castle walls and ends up with a beautiful refugee-camp worker.

We promise to deliver more exciting new titles in the coming year. Make it your New Year's resolution to read them all!

Happy reading!

Mary-Theresa Hussey

Mary-Theresa Hussey
Senior Editor

Please address questions and book requests to:
Silhouette Reader Service
U.S.: 3010 Walden Ave., P.O. Box 1325, Buffalo, NY 14269
Canadian: P.O. Box 609, Fort Erie, Ont. L2A 5X3

The Makeover Takeover

SANDRA PAUL

SILHOUETTE *Romance*

Published by Silhouette Books

America's Publisher of Contemporary Romance

Special thanks and acknowledgment are given
to Sandra Paul for her contribution to the
HAVING THE BOSS'S BABY series.

Dedicated with love to
Nikki and Dano.
Thanks for all the help and encouragement.

 SILHOUETTE BOOKS

ISBN 0-373-19559-1

THE MAKEOVER TAKEOVER

Books by Sandra Paul

Silhouette Romance

Last Chance for Marriage #883
The Reluctant Hero #1016
His Accidental Angel #1087
The Makeover Takeover #1559

Silhouette Yours Truly

Baby on the Way

Harlequin Duets

Head Over Heels
Baby Bonus?
Moonstruck

SANDRA PAUL

married her high school sweetheart and they live in Southern California with their three children, their dog and their cat.

She loves to travel, even if it's just several trips a month to her hometown bookstore. Bookstores are her favorite place to be.

Her first book with Silhouette Romance was the winner of RWA Golden Heart Award and a finalist for an RWA RITA Award.

Note to self: Who's having my baby?

Trudy—hopeless romantic, office gossip, can't keep a secret. *If it's not her, she might know who it is!*

Lauren Connor—dates a lot, trying out new looks to impress her boss, was out sick with stomach flu. *Hmm...*

~~Sharon Davies~~—recently trapped in an elevator with a major client, blushes whenever he's around, looking a little green lately. *Could she be carrying my baby?*

Leila—makes eyes at me. *Is it more than a crush?*

Maggie Steward—my personal assistant, wants children, clock is ticking. *She would never go to a sperm bank!*

Julia Parker—worries that her endometriosis could make her infertile. No man in her life. *Definite sperm bank material!*

~~Jennifer Martin~~—eight months pregnant. Is it her late fiancé's baby? *Is it mine?*

WHEN THE LIGHTS WENT OUT... October 2001
A PREGNANT PROPOSAL November 2001
THE MAKEOVER TAKEOVER December 2001
LAST CHANCE FOR BABY January 2002
SHE'S HAVING MY BABY! February 2002

KANE HALEY, INC.
Chicago, IL

Chapter One

"C'mon, Lauren."

"No."

"Why not? We have plenty of time…."

"No, we do not." Sitting stiffly erect in her chair, Lauren Connor carefully avoided meeting her boss's eyes across the wide expanse of his oak desk. Focusing on the slice of the Chicago skyline visible in the window beyond his broad shoulder, she added, "Mr. Haley might be here at any moment and the last thing I want is for the head of the company to catch us fooling around."

"He's not due for at least another thirty minutes—"

"Twenty."

"Twenty then. That's time enough." Rafe Mitchell studied his secretary's unrelenting expression, then coaxed, "C'mon, Lauren, it'll help me relax. This Bartlett deal is really stressing me out."

Unable to stop herself, Lauren stole a glance at his face. His dark eyes met hers, and her stomach flipped in a way that had nothing to do with the nausea that had been plaguing her all morning. Breaking away from that intent stare, she pushed her glasses higher on the bridge of her nose and let her gaze wander over him, trying to assess the truth of his claim.

He certainly didn't look stressed. As usual, he was leaning back in his chair with his long legs stretched out in front of him and his hands thrust into the pockets of his custom-tailored gray suit. But maybe he *was* feeling the pressure. No one knew better than she how stressful working at the accounting firm of Kane Haley, Inc., could be, and heaven knew, as Vice-President of Mergers and Acquisitions, Rafe had more than his share of challenges.

On the other hand, no one else knew better than she did how good Rafe was at getting his own way. Even the absurdly hopeful expression he'd donned couldn't hide the stubborn determination indelibly marked in the hard lines of his face. Rafe Mitchell was tough, and he looked it—from the tight, muscular build of his six-foot-tall body to the shrewd, cynical intelligence gleaming in his dark-brown eyes.

Catching a glimpse of amusement in their depths, Lauren's spine stiffened even more. "Well, it doesn't relax me," she said, trying to make her soft voice sound firm and implacable. "All I end up with is a lot of frustration."

"That won't happen this time—I promise," Rafe said quickly.

She looked at her notepad, pushing her glasses back up as they slipped down her nose again. She doodled on the paper, pretending to add more items to the list she'd made.

"I'll even let you go first."

Her pen faltered. To her inner disgust, Lauren could feel herself weakening. She bit her lip, trying not to give in.

His deep voice turned husky with persuasion. "*Please,* Laurie..."

The last of her resolution crumbled. In the three years she'd worked for Rafe, she never *had* been able to resist that half-demanding, half-coaxing tone—so why did she think today would be any different? Especially when she wasn't feeling well enough to deal with him.

She slapped her notepad down on his desk. "All right— you win. I'll play you one game—but just one! And for heaven's sake, let's make it quick."

Triumph flashed across Rafe's face, and he sprang to his feet. "Great! You sit at my desk. I'll set things up."

Lauren walked over and settled into his chair. The supple leather still retained the warmth from his body, and she sighed as the heat comforted her, helping to dispel the small shivers chasing along her limbs. Even the thick brown sweater and long wool skirt she was wearing weren't helping much to keep her warm today.

She wrapped her arms around her middle as another pain tightened the muscles in her stomach. She couldn't be coming down with the flu—not now. The niggling thought that it might be something else, something even more serious, she pushed right out of her mind. She didn't have time to deal with any personal problems. There was too much work to be done. The meeting with Mr. Haley this morning, the future meetings she needed to set up to prepare for the Bartlett takeover. Contracts to get ready, decorations to plan for the company Christmas party—the list was endless. And right at the top of it was trying to handle a boss who insisted on wasting valuable time.

She watched Rafe as he paced off approximately seven feet on the plush cream carpet. He placed his empty trash can on the spot. Then he strode back toward her to retrieve a small orange hoop, complete with a net, from a drawer in his desk.

Lauren shook her head at the satisfaction on his face as

he crouched to attach it to the rim of the can. "Don't you ever get tired of playing these silly games?"

"Nope," he answered, without bothering to look up from his task. "I like to win."

"You'll probably end up with ulcers," Lauren told him morosely, the thought prompted by another wave of nausea. "You're much too competitive."

Rafe slanted his secretary an amused glance. If that wasn't the pot calling the kettle black, he didn't know what was. Lauren was competitive, too. She just didn't know it.

Not many other people would realize it at first glance either. She was definitely a girl who would have played with Barbies and tea sets with her mother, rather than sports with her dad. Everything about her was, well…sort of wimpy. She wore glasses that constantly slipped down the bridge of her small nose. The thick lenses gave her blue-gray eyes a slightly surprised look—like an anxious little mole, blinking in the sunshine. Her mouth was unremarkable, and her thin face and pale cheeks were framed by straight brown hair.

Her movements were precise, her attitude was prim. She didn't talk about herself much, but Rafe knew her father had died when she was five or so. As a result, she wasn't used to the rather crude way men could talk—never mind understanding the way they thought. Nor did she have even the slightest clue about the purpose, rules, or even the star players of the games men loved. Not football, hockey, baseball—not any game for that matter. Rafe had discovered that amazing fact barely a week after she started working for him. He'd mentioned Michael Jordan—who could grow up in Illinois and not know about Mike?—and been totally stunned when she'd asked in all sincerity if Jordan worked in the mail room.

Rafe had known right then and there that his new secretary needed help. She needed to get out more. She needed to quit being so serious all the time and so polite. To loosen up a little, build some confidence and learn to survive in the big city. Most of all, as part of his takeover team, she needed to develop some fighting spirit. And nothing was better for achieving all of those goals, Rafe knew, than a little healthy competition.

Hadn't playing football and baseball kept him out of trouble when he was in high school? Major trouble, anyway. Hadn't the boxing, the hand-to-hand fighting workouts—the all-night poker games—kept him sharp and aggressive, not to mention solvent, during his stint in the marines? Of course they had. And once he'd gotten his degree on a GI bill, hadn't his ability to play the corporate game—not to let up on a deal until he had the terms he was after—eventually landed him this job with Kane Haley, Inc.? You'd better believe it.

So—being the great guy he was—he'd taken Lauren under his wing. Every couple months or so, he'd introduced her to a new game, to broaden her experience and help to de-wimp her. She'd learned about hockey by playing "mint hockey" on his desk, using a hard candy for the puck and pencils as their hockey sticks. For tennis, he'd strung up a tiny net of paper clips, and they'd batted a wad of paper back and forth. They'd tackled soccer, baseball—but his favorite game so far was trash-can basketball. Now *there* was a game that required skill.

Not that Lauren had any. Her depth perception was dismal and her coordination sucked. Still, he couldn't help believing she had to have potential for something, he reflected as he pulled out the orange foam ball he'd stashed in a potted fern near the window. She was slim for her height of about five foot six or so, and had nice long legs.

Her build at least looked athletic enough—until you put her to the test.

He tossed her the ball, then shook his head as she reached out awkwardly and fumbled the catch. Pathetic—simply pathetic.

But her lack of talent wouldn't stop her from giving the contest her best shot, he knew. Lauren always balked at participating at first—she had completely outdated notions about correct behavior at work—but once he'd bullied, cajoled or tricked her into playing, her competitive nature would rise to the fore. She hated to lose, and entered each of the ridiculous contests with a fierce determination to win.

Rafe hid a slight grin. Already she was frowning over his placement of the basket, her slim brows drawing down over her eyes.

"Isn't that farther away than you set it last time?" she asked doubtfully, pushing up her glasses as she glanced at him.

"No."

"But—Rafe!" Her frown deepened as he shrugged out of his jacket. "What are you doing? Mr. Haley—"

"Doesn't give a damn how I'm dressed, as long as I get the job done—and I do. Every time." Rafe lifted his brows, studying her disapproving face as he began to roll up his white shirtsleeves. "Surely you don't expect me to play a serious game in my suit?"

"Why not? You know you'll beat me with or without it."

She made the last comment almost beneath her breath, but Rafe heard it anyway. Like *his* coordination, his hearing was excellent. He gave her a reproachful look. "Hey, don't I always give you a sporting chance?" She opened her mouth, but before she could reply, he interjected, "Of course, I do. I'll shoot at double the distance."

"Like that's going to matter," Lauren grumbled, but he could tell he had her hooked. She made a practice motion with the ball toward the can before adding, "I think you just like to make me play because then you can always win."

Rafe suppressed another smile at the faint disgust in her voice. It wasn't like Lauren to complain. She usually participated in each contest in resigned silence.

He prudently kept his mouth shut, although he could have told her it wasn't beating her that he enjoyed so much, but rather watching the fierce determination she put into the games. Like now, for instance. She'd forgotten all about Kane Haley's imminent arrival and had abandoned that aloof, grave expression she seemed to feel lately was appropriate as his secretary. Instead, her face was screwed up in a fierce scowl of concentration, her eyes narrowed behind her glasses as she visually measured the distance to the goal.

He let her study it for a few seconds longer, then prompted, "Ready?"

She nodded, her long, straight brown hair swinging gently against her cheek. "Ready."

She lifted the ball. Just as she was just about to release it, he said, "Wait!"

Lauren almost lurched out of her chair. She gasped, her blue-gray eyes wide with alarm, her glasses askew on her small nose. "What? What's wrong?" She straightened her glasses and glanced nervously at the door. "Is Mr. Haley coming?"

"Nah. We just forgot to make a bet."

Her eyes narrowed again—on him this time. "I don't want to bet. I keep telling you, betting is illegal."

"Now would I suggest doing something illegal?" Her expression said yes, but before she could answer, he did it for her. "Of course not," he said smoothly. "I was just thinking of a simple, friendly wager—maybe for a small exchange of services."

She still looked suspicious. "What services?"

"Oh, I don't know…" He pretended to consider a moment. "How about if you win, I make a Christmas donation to the women's shelter you're collecting for. A *hefty* donation." No need to tell her, he decided, that the check was already made out and ready to be donated in either case. The incentive would spur her on.

Sure enough, her eyes lit up, then turned wary again. "And if I lose…."

"If you lose, then all you have to do is a little Christmas shopping for me. Pick up something for a few of my friends."

"What friends?"

"Oh, I dunno. Maybe Amy. And Maureen. And possibly Nancy."

Now she really looked disapproving—and definitely torn. Rafe kept his expression serious with an effort. He'd asked her last week to pick up some gifts for the women he was currently dating, and she'd responded with a stiff little speech about "gift-giving being a personal thing" and "not feeling right about doing it for him" and how she was sure "his friends would rather have something he'd chosen himself." He'd listened and agreed, but hell, he had no idea what to get women, and he hated buying gifts anyway.

It would be much better all around if Lauren just did it for him.

He knew he wasn't actually giving her any choice; the women's shelter was a big deal to Lauren. She really got into stuff like that. Charities. Church. The new child-care facility Maggie Steward, Kane's administrative assistant, was adding to the corporation. Anything she felt would help make someone's life better always caught Lauren's attention. No way on earth would she be able to refuse a possible donation.

But he asked her anyway, "So whaddaya say? Just get them whatever women like. Throw it all on my credit card."

"Fine," she answered, gritting her small white teeth.

Now he'd *really* riled her up. She pressed her lips together and picked up a pen. She deliberately wrote down a line on her notepad, and even took the time to scribble something in the margin.

Finished finally, she threw down her pen. She glared at him, then glared back at the basket. Jabbing at her glasses, she set her delicate jaw and pushed up the sleeves of her brown sweater. She even wiggled forward to perch at the extreme edge of the chair, tugging down the hem of her brown plaid skirt as it inched up above her knees.

Settled into position, she lifted her arm again. With a mighty scowl and a jerky flip of her wrist, she released the ball.

The orange missile shot straight toward the basket and plopped down—three feet short.

Rafe wanted to howl at the frustration on her face. She was stiff as a baseball bat now with her hands clenched into small fists by her sides. But instead of laughing, he shook his head in mock commiseration. "Ah, damn. That's too bad," he said sympathetically. He scooped the ball up from the carpet. "Let's see if I can do any better."

He made a minor production of measuring off his shooting range, making sure he doubled the distance Lauren had thrown from. Then with a casual toss, he threw the ball.

He nodded in satisfaction as it sank right in the can. Man, he was good. He glanced at his secretary to see if she fully appreciated his prowess, and his smile disappeared.

Lauren looked sick. Her pale skin had a yellow cast and as he watched, she flinched, then wrapped her arms around her waist.

"Are you okay?" he asked.

"Of course," she said, but the words ended on a small gasp. "I just have a small pain in my stomach."

He frowned as she tightened her arms again. "What do you mean pain?" he demanded. "Like appendicitis?"

"No. Really—I'm fine."

"There's a flu bug going around—"

"It's nothing," she insisted, dismissing his concern with an airy wave of her hand.

A second later, however, she clasped that same hand over her mouth, her eyes widening in alarm. Jumping up, she looked frantically at the trash can—still decked out with its silly net—then dashed out the door.

Chapter Two

When Lauren emerged from the women's restroom a few minutes later, she was feeling much better. She'd splashed cold water on her face, rinsed out her mouth, and was sure she could make it through the rest of the day. But then she saw Rafe leaning against the wall outside with his arms crossed, wearing his black overcoat. Her brown coat and scarf were slung over his arm, and he had the scuffed brown messenger bag she used as a purse clutched in his big hand.

He straightened at the sight of her. "Okay, let's go," he said briskly, before she could speak. "You're sick and I'm taking you home."

"I'm not sick," Lauren said, automatically reaching for her bag.

He relinquished it, but turned her this way and that as he hooked her arms into her coat and tugged it up her shoulders. Then, taking her arm in a firm grasp, he steered her down the hall toward the elevators.

"Rafe—wait! I'm better now," Lauren told him, trying to dig in her heels.

"Glad to hear it," he replied, but kept walking, pulling her along with him.

When they reached the elevator, he still didn't give her a chance to argue, pushing the button and pulling her inside before she could think of a way to convince him she was all right.

The doors closed and he turned to face her. "You're white as a ghost, Lauren." Ignoring her protests, he slung the scarf around her neck. He wrapped it around and around to the mellow rendition of "Jingle Bells" seeping from the elevator speakers. "I'm taking you home. I don't want you driving yourself."

Lauren pulled down the wool folds stacked up over her nose. "But there's no need! Mr. Haley—"

"Will understand. I left him a message explaining that you weren't feeling well. Since it's Friday, you'll have the entire weekend to rest up."

Lauren opened her mouth to protest again, then shut it as she glanced at Rafe's face. His tone sounded pleasant enough, but the look in his eyes told her he meant what he said.

Lauren sighed, subsiding back into her scarf. She'd seen that look before, whenever he was working on a deal. Rafe was determined to get his way, and any argument she made would simply be a waste of breath.

She decided to try anyway. "I can take a taxi. Or the bus. Or maybe Jay will give me a ride home."

He glanced down at her, raising his brows in question. "Who's Jay?"

"Jay Leonardo, the neighbor who drove me in this morning."

"What's wrong with your car?" he asked, as the elevator lurched to a stop at the fourteenth floor. The mirrored doors slid open for another passenger.

"I'm not sure," Lauren told him. "It was slow starting and Jay offered—"

"Why, *hello* Rafe," a sultry voice interrupted.

Lauren looked up. A blond woman was standing at the open doors, staring at Rafe with delight.

His crooked grin appeared. "Well, hello, Nancy," he drawled.

The blonde slid into the elevator and immediately slunk up next to Rafe. Like a snake, Lauren decided. A busty one.

So this was the Nancy she was supposed to buy a present for.

Lauren faced forward as the door closed. Beside her, Rafe and the woman exchanged pleasantries as "Jingle Bells" ended and "White Christmas" began. Trying to avoid looking in the mirrors surrounding her, Lauren glanced up at the overhead lights, then down at her unvarnished nails. But finally she gave in. She might as well be invisible, she thought, staring at their reflections in the mirrored door.

Rafe stood next to her, but he wasn't looking at her; not at all. He'd fixed his entire attention on the woman on his other side—and the blonde's was fixed entirely on him.

Which, of course, was no surprise in either case. The woman looked beautiful in her expensive blue suit, fitted within an inch of her life. Flimsy-looking heels showcased her tiny feet, and a fur hung over her arm. Sleek, sophisticated, she had at least ten years on Lauren's twenty-four and radiated the confidence those years had obviously given her. And as for Rafe...

Lauren studied him, noting how his crisp white shirt made his hair and eyes look even darker. How the tailored lines of his charcoal suit contrasted sharply with his rugged face. He smiled briefly at the newcomer and his straight teeth gleamed. Beguiling creases appeared in his lean cheeks.

Rafe looked...just fine, too.

Lauren looked away from him to stare woodenly ahead at her own image. With her frumpy cloth coat, striped scarf, and serviceable low pumps—and her long brown hair hanging down in a tangle around her glasses—she looked like a stump. A furry, brown one.

"What are you doing in this area of town?" Rafe was asking Nancy.

"I had an appointment with my accountant on the four-teenth floor and thought I'd stop by your office to see if you wanted to have lunch. I haven't heard from you for a while," the woman murmured in a chiding tone, looking up at him from beneath long lashes.

Ooh, bad move, Lauren thought. Rafe didn't encourage his dates to visit him at the office. It made them territorial, he'd once told Lauren. Sure enough, the expression in his eyes cooled. But he answered pleasantly enough, "Yeah, I've been pretty busy at work."

The blonde pressed again. "You still have my number, don't you?" She reached out and lightly touched his arm.

Rafe lifted a brow. "It's on my speed dial," he assured her.

Lauren tried to turn her sudden snort into the semblance of a cough. "Sorry," she mumbled, as they both glanced at her in the mirror.

Rafe's gaze met hers. She quickly looked away as his eyes narrowed a little, but could feel his gaze still on her.

"This is my secretary," he announced suddenly, as if he'd just remembered she was in the elevator, too. He put his arm around Lauren's shoulders to turn her toward them. "I think you've spoken with her on the phone. Lauren, Nancy. Nance—Lauren."

Lauren politely stuck out her hand. The blonde had reluctantly grasped it, when Rafe added, "I'm afraid I'm going to have to pass on lunch today. I'm taking Lauren home. She's been sick—vomiting and all that."

Heat swept up Lauren's face as the other woman snatched her hand away. Nancy stepped back, glanced around the mirrored box as if looking for a way out, then jabbed at the panel.

The elevator jolted to a stop. "I need to—ah, get out here," the blonde said, edging around Lauren. With a final, "See you, Rafe. Call me!" she disappeared down the hall.

Rafe pushed a button. The doors slid shut again. A distressingly upbeat version of "Sleigh Ride" came on. Lauren glared at Rafe's pseudo-innocent look in the mirror, and her hands clenched by her sides. "I'd appreciate it," she said icily, "if you wouldn't use me as some kind of blonde repellent."

His eyes crinkled in amusement, but his tone was reproachful as he asked, "Now would I do something like that?"

"Yes!" Annoyed with his antics, Lauren turned toward the panel. "And I have better things to do than to fool around, so if you don't mind, I'd like to get back to the office and—"

He caught her hand to prevent her pushing the button just as the elevator shuddered to another stop. The doors slid open on the street level. Rafe latched on to her arm. He marched her through the lobby and out of the main entrance into the crisp December air.

Horns blared, traffic roared by on the busy street in front of them. A Salvation Army Santa rang his bell with incessant cheerfulness in front of the building next door, making Lauren wince. Rafe paused on the sidewalk a moment to tug her scarf up over her ears, pushing her hands aside when she tried to stop him. Then, satisfied with his efforts at keeping her warm, he took her arm again, urging her toward the parking structure.

Lauren's feet slipped a little on the icy pavement. His grip on her arm tightened to steady her.

"You should have worn your boots," he murmured, glancing disapprovingly at her low heels.

Lauren spat out her scarf and raised her chin as far as possible to tell him, "You didn't give me the chance! They're under my desk." If that wasn't just like the man, she fumed, retreating back into the wool as the cold Chicago wind nipped her nose. To blame her when he was the one at fault....

He caught her hand as she slid again, and wrapped his other arm around her waist. Tucking her under his shoulder, he almost carried her across the frozen sidewalk. "And what about your gloves?" He raised his brows and gently squeezed her cold fingers with his warm ones for emphasize. "Are those at your desk, too?"

Lauren pressed her lips together. He knew they weren't; he'd scolded her for not wearing them when she'd come in that morning. So she decided not to answer that question, concentrating instead on trying to keep her balance.

When they reached his sleek black car, she did try to tell him once again that she could get home without his help, but he ignored her, unlocking the door to stuff her gently but firmly inside.

Knowing there was no changing his mind, Lauren crossed her arms and watched the city roll past the window. When he slid a disk into his CD player, she gave him a sidelong glance. Music pulsed from his speakers, a heavy rock song, and he tapped on the steering wheel to the beat.

Her eyes lingered for a moment on his hands, following the movement of his long fingers. Her gaze slid up to his face, following the sharp angle of his jaw up his cheekbone to his eyes. His dark lashes half shielded his gaze, which were fixed on the road ahead as he cut through traffic. As always, he looked completely confident, sure of where he was going and what he wanted.

She knew she didn't need to give him directions to her apartment. After all, Rafe was the one who'd found it for her. A short time after she became his secretary he'd condemned her first place sight unseen as being in a "dangerous" area. He'd then recommended her present address which he considered much safer; Rafe had grown up in the city, and he knew his Chicago. The rent for the converted Victorian was a little more than Lauren had wanted to spend, but after listening to his horror stories about her first location for an entire week, she'd ended up plunking down the money with a minimum of fuss.

Obviously pleased with his victory, Rafe had helped her move. But then he hadn't come around again until the Christmas season, when he'd turned up on her doorstep with a tree for her. He'd arrived with one last year, too, and Lauren wondered if he planned to do the same this Christmas. She was trying to think of a polite way to ask—without making it sound as if she *expected* him to buy her a tree—when they pulled up before her building.

Lauren sighed in relief, thankful the short drive was over. Now he could get back to work. She turned to him as she opened her door. "I really appreciate—"

"You sit right there," he ordered, switching off the engine. "I'm taking you up."

The house had been divided into four apartments; Lauren's was one of two on the second story. As they climbed the outside stairs that had been added to provide a separate entrance, she worriedly tried to remember if she'd straightened up that morning—or if she'd left the place a mess. Probably, the latter, she thought gloomily. She hadn't felt very well this morning, or last night either for that matter.

She paused on the landing with her key in hand, hoping to head Rafe off. "Thank you for—"

"Here, give me that," he interrupted, removing the key from her grasp. In less than five seconds he'd opened the door, nudged her inside, and followed right behind her.

Lauren entered reluctantly. Her gaze darted around as she struggled to remove the wool tourniquet Rafe had tied around her neck. The apartment had an open design with the kitchen, dining and living rooms all combined into one big living area. The place didn't look too bad, she decided, glancing toward the kitchen. She'd left a couple of cupboard doors open and her breakfast dishes were in the sink, but no big deal.

Relieved, she looked up at Rafe to try to thank him again, and caught him staring at her folded laundry, piled on a nearby chair. Right on top of the pile was her white cotton, size 34A bra.

A hot flush crept up her face. Lauren sidled over to the chair, intending to tuck her bra beneath her other clothes. But just as she picked it up, Rafe took off again.

"Where's your thermostat?" he asked, striding across the living room. "It's in the hall, isn't it? Let's get the heat up in here."

He disappeared down her hallway, and Lauren hurried after him. She caught up with him by the thermostat located next to her bedroom door—her open bedroom door. Lauren groaned as she glanced inside. Her bed was unmade, her flannel nightgown was thrown across the sheets and her underwear was on the floor.

She yanked the door closed, blocking Rafe's view of the rumpled bed and the rest of the messy room.

He didn't seem to notice. He adjusted her thermostat to his satisfaction and turned to go back into the living room. Lauren followed, noting in relief that he was *finally* heading to the door.

He waited in her tiny foyer for her to catch up. When she reached his side, Lauren took a deep breath to restore her composure, and said in as calm a voice as she could manage, "Thank you for driving me home."

"You're welcome," he responded, his tone as solemn as hers. "Do you want to go to bed?"

Lauren gasped, her startled gaze flying to meet his. "*No!* I mean, *yes.* I mean—I'll do that—just as soon as you leave."

Unholy amusement lit his dark eyes. Lauren's face burned hotter than ever. Of course he hadn't meant the question the way that it had sounded. As if *he* was planning to go to bed with her. What was wrong with her today?

Instinctively, she lifted her hands to cover her red cheeks, then yanked them down again as she realized she was still holding her bra. She whipped it behind her back again, shutting her eyes in embarrassment. Rafe would tease the life out of her now—he loved to tease every chance he got—and, heaven knew, she'd just given him plenty of ammunition. She lifted her lashes and stared up at him in dread, waiting mutely for him to start.

But he didn't. Maybe it was the apprehension on her face or maybe he took pity on her because he thought she had the flu. Maybe he simply remembered Mr. Haley was probably waiting back at the office.

Whatever the reason, Rafe merely told her, "Well, I'm leaving now, so go climb in between the sheets."

He reached for the doorknob, then paused. He turned back to face her and tilted up her chin, forcing her to meet his gaze. "And forget about coming into work on Monday if you still feel sick. That's an order, Lauren."

He released her and left. Lauren bolted the door behind him and sagged against it in relief, her skin still tingling from his touch.

Rafe was still chuckling to himself as he strode down the hall to his office. He'd never seen Lauren so flustered. What a kick she could be sometimes, getting all upset and embarrassed simply because she'd left a bra out. Did she think he'd never seen one before?

He forgot about Lauren's amusing modesty, though, when he entered his office to find the president of the firm waiting. Kane Haley was sitting on the edge of Rafe's desk, his broad shoulders hunched as he frowned down at a paper in his hand.

Rafe shrugged out of his overcoat, tossing it on the rack by the door, then moved forward to greet the other man. "Kane—have you been waiting long? Didn't you get my message?"

"That's why I waited," his boss replied, rising to his feet. "How's Lauren?"

"Lauren?" Rafe shrugged, faintly surprised by the question. "She's sick, as I said."

Kane looked back down at the paper, and Rafe realized it was his own scrawled message that the other man was holding. "You say here," Kane said, "that she has a stom-achache."

"She does." Surely Kane didn't think Lauren had lied

simply to go home early? "She wasn't faking, if that's what you think."

"I don't." Kane dropped the slip of paper down on the desk. He paced to the window—skirting the trash can that Rafe had left in the middle of the carpet—and stood silently for a long moment, looking out at the view. Then he drew a deep breath, and turned, meeting Rafe's eyes.

"What I think," Kane said slowly, "is that Lauren might be pregnant."

Chapter Three

"Pregnant?" Rafe stared at the other man in disbelief. Lauren? *His* secretary Lauren—pregnant? "Where on earth did you get a crazy idea like that?"

"You said in your note her stomach was bothering her."

"Yeah, so—"

"Has she been tired a lot? Fatigued in the mornings? Has she seemed moody at all?"

Rafe paused, his chest tightening. She had seemed more serious and distracted lately. Even kind of droopy at times. His voice sharpened, "Yeah, but she's probably picked up that flu bug that's been going around."

Kane frowned. "Did she seem to have any other flu symptoms? A headache? Fever?"

Rafe remembered how cool Lauren's hands had felt and the pale color of her cheeks—before she'd blushed so furiously, that was. Now that he thought about it, she *hadn't* appeared to have any other flu symptoms. Could she be—?

Ridiculous. Hell, what was he thinking?

"That certainly doesn't mean she's pregnant." Exasperated with himself as well as Kane for considering the idea, even for a second, Rafe gave a short laugh. "Lauren's not even dating anyone. Who's supposed to have fathered this mythical child?"

"Me."

The whole conversation—odd from the beginning—suddenly made sense to Rafe. Too much sense.

His jaw tightened. He'd always liked Kane. Had found him to be an intelligent and fair man to work for. And he knew the guy had a pretty active social life. But to do something like this....

Rafe's voice lowered to a deceptively even tone. "Are you saying," he asked carefully, "that you've slept with *Lauren?*"

"Hell, no!" Kane looked shocked, then honestly appalled. "I've never even touched the woman." He met Rafe's hard gaze, and his own narrowed in response. "So if you're thinking of trying to throw a punch at me, you can just forget it."

Until that moment, Rafe hadn't realized he'd assumed a fighting stance, with his fists clenched and his legs braced aggressively. "Hell." He thrust his hands into his pockets. "If you didn't sleep with her, then how could she be having your baby?"

"She might not be—at least, I'm not sure...." Kane paced across the carpet to stare unseeingly out the window again. "The fact of the matter is, *someone* at this firm is pregnant with my child. All I'm trying to do is find out who she is."

The silence stretched. Then Kane turned around. He studied Rafe's expression a second, and a smile twisted his mouth. "Don't look at me like that either. I'm not insane—not yet, anyway," he said wryly. His expression turned grim again. "Do you remember my friend—Bill Jeffers? The one who had cancer?"

Rafe raised his brows at the sudden change of subject, but nodded. Yeah, he remembered Jeffers. The guy hadn't been much older than he himself—or Kane for that matter.

"When Bill first found out he was sick," Kane continued, "he decided to go to the Lakeside Reproductive Clinic to make a sperm deposit to ensure that if the radiation treatment affected him adversely, he could still have kids. I went along with him to provide support and a—well, a back-up donation—in case he needed it."

With a sigh, Kane trod across the carpet again. "Thankfully, he didn't. In fact, he's fine, and his wife is pregnant—by the usual methods I might add—and their baby is due in June."

"I'm happy for them." And he was, Rafe thought, fighting back his growing tension. But it was all he could do to keep his voice even as he said, "But what does all this have to do with Lauren?"

"Nothing. Or maybe everything." Kane ran his hand wearily through his dark hair. "You see, after Bill called to tell me his wife was pregnant, I contacted the clinic to have my own donation *un*donated, so to speak, only to find out it was too late. It seems the clinic goofed—bigtime. My donation has already been used, and by a woman at this firm. Someone on the clinic staff saw Kane Haley, Inc., on her insurance form and thought my sperm was being requested."

Rafe could feel the back of his neck prickle as the short hairs there literally stood on end. "Holy sh—"

"—*exactly*," Kane said grimly. "And now the clinic is refusing to tell me who the woman is, citing a lot of legalese about her right to privacy—never mind my right to know who's bearing my child. Anyway, I'm lining up a lawyer to get to the bottom of things, but until then...well, to be truthful, it's been hell. Have you ever noticed how many women work at this firm?''

Rafe started to nod.

"How many *fertile* women there are out there?"

Rafe changed his nod to a negative shake. That was the last thing he'd ever thought about. Kids weren't on his agenda at all.

He stood there silently as Kane rose and paced restlessly, skirting the trash can each time he passed. Kane added, "Every time one of the women around here puts on weight, or gets emotional—or complains of a stomachache—well, I can't help but wonder..."

"...if she's the one," Rafe concluded.

He pursed his lips in a silent whistle. Whoa. Talk about a good deed coming back to bite you on the butt. He glanced at Kane's haggard expression and silently shook his head. A situation like this would be hard on anyone, but it must be especially hard for a guy like Kane who obviously took his responsibilities seriously. Even, it seemed, his responsibility to a child he hadn't planned to help create.

But he doubted Kane would have much success in his search. "I think you're wasting your time," he warned him. "You'll probably never find her if she doesn't want to be found. And even if you do, she might not welcome your interference—especially if she's married."

"What if she isn't married? What if she's going to try to raise the kid—my kid—on her own, and she needs help? Or the child does? I can't just walk away and pretend it doesn't exist."

Rafe didn't know what to say about that, but he could set his boss's mind at ease on one point. He'd bet his—hell, he'd bet his *Porsche*—that his secretary wasn't the woman carrying that child. The tight feeling in his chest eased. "It's not Lauren," he said bluntly.

Kane swung around. "How do you know? Unless..." He slanted Rafe a considering glance. "Are you dating her?"

"No, of course not," Rafe said, surprised by the question. "She's a nice girl, but not the kind of woman I'd ever get involved with."

Kane still didn't seem convinced. "You're pretty protective of her."

"I'm not protective—not personally, anyway," Rafe told him, growing slightly annoyed. Couldn't a guy be concerned about a woman—about his own secretary—without people getting the wrong impression?

Apparently not, since Kane still looked skeptical. So Rafe explained, "It's just that her mother died soon after Lauren moved here—and she'd never lived on her own before. And Lauren's, well, she's sweet and kind of naive. Besides," he added, warming to his subject, "simply because I object to the thought of an older, experienced man taking advantage of an unsophisticated younger woman doesn't mean— What?" he demanded, as a smile crossed Kane's face. "Did I say something funny?"

"Not at all," Kane drawled, not bothering to hide his amusement. "But you must admit, coming from you..."

"What do you mean, coming from me?" Rafe frowned. "The women I get involved with all know the score upfront." He always made sure of that. No way did he want there to be any misunderstandings later on down the road.

"If you're not involved with Lauren, than how can you be so sure she's not pregnant?" Kane demanded, his expression turning serious again.

"Because Lauren isn't the kind of woman to go it alone—to try to raise a child without a father," Rafe replied, complete certainty in his voice. "Hell, Kane, I've worked with the woman almost every day for three years. She's as traditional as they come. If she wanted a baby, she'd get married first."

"Are you sure?"

"I'm sure she wouldn't head to a sperm bank to get the job done. She grew up without a father. We talked once about how difficult that can be on a child." At least, Lauren had talked about it. Remembering a couple of the heavy-handed foster fathers he'd lived with after his own mother had died when he was twelve, Rafe hadn't been quite as convinced.

But the firmness of his tone apparently convinced Kane that Lauren wasn't the woman he was searching for. Kane let the subject drop, and they moved onto a discussion about the latest takeover Rafe was orchestrating. It was clear, however, that Kane's mind wasn't on business, and soon Rafe suggested that they postpone the discussion until Lauren's return. Since it was Lauren's job to gather the numbers and analyze the data, they would save time if they waited for her.

Kane readily agreed. "We'll set up another meeting then," he said, rising to his feet. "When will she be back?"

"Probably Monday. From what I hear this bug doesn't last long," Rafe said deliberately, wanting to stress again that Lauren wasn't the sperm bank bandit Kane was searching for.

Kane studied him, an unreadable expression on his face. "Are you sure—"

"I am."

With a final nod of acknowledgment, Kane left the office, closing the door behind him.

Rafe walked over and sat behind his desk. Leaning back

in his chair, he stared at that closed door a while, filled with profound sympathy for the man—and equally profound thankfulness that he wasn't in Kane's shoes. He wondered what Kane planned to do if he ever found the woman and discovered that she did need help. Offer to support the kid? Maybe even marry her? Nah, Kane wasn't that crazy.

Catching sight of the message slip Kane had left on his desk, Rafe absently wadded it into a ball and tossed it toward the abandoned trash can. The paper sank without touching the rim. Not that he had anything against marriage. Not at all, Rafe thought, reaching for another scrap. He crumpled that up, too. Marriage was fine for other people. He supposed a wife could be an asset to a man's career. Especially a rich, well-born, attractive wife with plenty of connections, a category that Maureen, Amy or Nancy all fit into nicely.

But he personally had no intention of taking such a drastic step. He took aim at the can again. So he made sure to keep his pistol holstered for the most part, and, at the least, to put a silencer on before he shot. *He* certainly wasn't going to be trapped by one of his bullets going astray, as Kane's had done.

The second paper ball followed the first. Another clean shot, nothing but net.

Rafe frowned as he considered the matter. How could the clinic make a mistake? What if some woman had learned about Kane's "contribution" and asked for his sperm on purpose? After all, Kane was a rich and powerful man, and women had been using pregnancy for ages to trap men into proposing.

If so, then Lauren was definitely out of the running, he decided. He wasn't sure he'd convinced Kane, but Rafe had no doubts at all on the matter. He knew the woman—

hell, he knew her better than anyone. They'd talked quite a bit over the years; were pretty good friends, as well as boss and secretary. She would never do something like that. It just wasn't in her makeup to chase after a man. Lauren would never try to trap a guy into marriage.

Still, he could understand why Kane might have suspected her of wanting a baby. When one of the women had brought her newborn into the office a few weeks ago, Lauren's face had lit up like a kid's at Christmas. She'd fussed and cooed over the little one, and had even held it for a while—a rather risky move, in Rafe's opinion. Not only was the kid alarmingly tiny, it spit up more than a fountain in the park.

But Lauren hadn't minded. Yeah, there was something—not maternal exactly—but definitely nurturing about his secretary. A slight smile curved his lips, and he leaned back in his chair, putting his feet up on his desk. Hell, she even worried about him at times—that he was working too hard or might be tired. There was a kindness, a gentle way about Lauren, that made her seem like the sort of woman who should have a bunch of kids around her knees. Pulling at her with sticky little hands. Clamoring for attention.

Rafe grimaced. Talk about a nightmare. But Lauren would handle it—revel in it probably. No doubt she would have a baby some day—far, far in the future. But now? No way. As he'd told Kane, she didn't even date. Whenever he asked her to work late, she never had a moment's hesitation in complying. Besides, they'd been so busy lately, she wouldn't have had time to meet a man, even if she wanted to.

Although…Rafe frowned, lowering his feet and straightening up again…although it appeared she had met one guy at least. This Jay Leonardo person. Her neighbor.

He shrugged that off. Just because the guy gave her a ride to work, didn't mean she'd gone out with him. Surely she would have mentioned it if she had.

Restlessly, he looked around for one more paper to throw before he settled down to work. Since his desk was clear except for Lauren's notepad, he pulled that closer to tear off a sheet. But when he turned the pad over, he realized she'd made some kind of list on it. That figured; Lauren was always making lists. More than once he'd watched her tick off the items she'd compiled, smug satisfaction on her face as she made each mark.

To his amusement, he saw that this time she'd doodled little pictures next to each of the reminders she'd written down. In her small, compressed handwriting she'd written: *Take gifts to women's shelter.* Boxed presents were next to that one, each adorned with an elaborate bow.

Number two was *Buy decorations for company Christmas party,* surrounded by round balls he took to be ornaments.

The third item didn't appear to make much sense. *Don't forget the...* he squinted, trying to make the last two words out... *Barbie bottoms?* He didn't think so. *Booby battles?* Nope. He was pretty sure it wasn't that either.

The doodle beside it proved equally confusing, so his gaze dropped to number four on the list. *Buy a special present for Jay.* Rafe stared at the happy face beaming beside the words, and his amusement faded. So she was buying presents for the guy, was she? His eyes narrowed. Then she probably *was* dating him, after all.

His eyes narrowed even more as he scanned the final item, the one she'd scribbled down before playing basketball. *Buy presents for Rafe's women.* What did she mean by that? he thought, irritated by her phrasing. They weren't *his* women—not specifically, anyway. What did she think he was? Some kind of sheik or something? He might like to play the field, but he wasn't stupid enough to put too many players in the game at once. All three women were just friends and nothing more. At least, so far.

And what had she drawn next to the words? He turned the pad this way and that, then picked it up and held it closer, trying to make out the tiny picture. A cowboy with a lasso? Santa with a whip? He stiffened as he realized there were horns on Santa's head. She'd drawn a devil, dammit, with its tail curling around to the front. Ending up in a place no tail had any business to be!

He leaned back, slightly stunned, unable to take his eyes off the offensive little stick figure cavorting in the margin. What the hell was this all about? he wondered, his annoyance growing even stronger. Okay, maybe he had virtually forced her to agree to buy the women gifts—but that didn't make him Satan, for heaven's sake! Never would he have believed Lauren could—would—draw something so downright graphic.

But since she had, that made booby battles a definite possibility, he decided, his gaze returning to number three. Both indecipherable words definitely began with B and— Ah, yes! The squiggle next to them was a *bottle*. Now he had it! *Don't forget the Barbie bottles.* What the…? Damn. That still didn't make any sense.

He studied the words once more. Suddenly, his stomach turned, as if the flu bug scurrying around the office had just attacked with a vengeance. That first word wasn't *Barbie* but…*baby*. His jaw tightened as he read the sentence again.

Don't forget the baby bottles.

By six that evening, Lauren was feeling much better. The thick, chalky pink medicine she'd forced down had soothed her upset stomach, and a long afternoon nap had done much to soothe her upset nerves.

She even felt well enough when she awoke to straighten the apartment. Once that chore was finished, she took a long hot shower then donned a comfortable sweat suit and slippers to lounge around in.

Feeling clean and cozy, she wandered into the kitchen and made herself a cup of tea, sipping it as she stared out the kitchen window. Dusk had already fallen, and lights from nearby houses gleamed through the barren trees and darkness. The view blurred as steam condensed on her glasses. Slipping them off, Lauren laid them on the counter, then realized the window was hazy, too.

She set down her cup. Leaning forward, she reached out to draw a Christmas tree in the mist. The freezing cold pane burned then numbed her fingertip. Outside, snow-flakes pelted against the glass in a brief, desperate flurry. But inside her apartment she was warm and safe…and alone.

Her hand dropped. Lauren stared at her drawing as it slowly disappeared into the mist again. She liked being alone, she told herself. She was used to it. Even as a child, she'd been something of an introvert—*my little dreamer,* her mother used to call her. She'd always felt more content with her books, her own thoughts and daydreams, than hanging out with a crowd.

Of course, she hadn't been completely alone then; she'd had her mother. Most people had at least some family— parents, siblings, even an aunt or an uncle or two. Or they were married by her age. Sharon Davies in accounting was only a year older, and she'd recently married a handsome widower. Jennifer Holder was near her age, and she'd re-cently tied the knot, too, and already had a baby. Most of the other single women at work at least had a lover. She had no one.

But just because a person was alone didn't mean that they were lonely, she reminded herself. She straightened her shoulders and picked up her cup. Take Rafe, for instance. Like her, he'd lost both parents, although he'd lost them much, much younger than she had. Rafe wasn't married either—and he liked it that way. Not that anyone could ever call him an introvert. He enjoyed women—lots of women.

She sipped her tea, the taste warm and bitter on her tongue, as she wondered who he'd be taking out that night. She'd never met the other two women he was currently dating. Still, judging by Nancy—and from the women he'd dated in the past—Lauren had a pretty fair idea of what they must be like.

For one thing, they were probably older than she was. Rafe preferred dating women who were near his own age of thirty-two, or even a little older. Most likely they'd be wealthy, and she had no doubt at all that, again like Nancy, they'd be beautiful. Not pretty or cute, but striking, with the polished, sleek appearance of women who had unlimited time and money to spend enhancing their looks.

What would it feel like, Lauren mused, to look like that? To know that when you entered a room, men's heads turned? She sighed, turning on the tap to clean out her cup. She couldn't even imagine it. Men just never responded to her that way. Most of the men she knew treated her like a pal, a buddy, a little sister. Or even a generic mixture of all three. The way Rafe did.

No, Rafe wasn't aware of her as a woman at all. She rinsed the cup slowly, letting the warm water flow over her cold fingers. So how could she have thought—even for a second—that he was asking her to sleep with him? Wincing in remembered embarrassment, she turned off the tap and set the cup on the drainer. Still, there was no sense worrying about it, she decided in an effort to comfort herself as she dried off her hands. She was sure he'd forgotten all about the incident—forgotten all about her—as soon as he got back to the office. Probably before he'd even reached his car.

She threw the towel down on the counter. So what if he had? And why was she thinking about him anyway? Probably he hadn't gone on a date at all, but had headed to the gym. Rafe was always up for a game of racquetball to release some of his energy.

Feeling restless herself suddenly, she headed into the living area. This room was her favorite all year round, but she especially liked it during the holidays since it looked so very Christmasy. Forest-green rugs were scattered on the gleaming hardwood floors, and she'd positioned her overstuffed burgundy couches to face each other in front of the small hearth, where a fire burned cheerily. She walked over to one of the couches. Pushing aside the teddy bear reposing in her favorite spot, she sat down and picked up her knitting.

She realized she'd left her glasses in the kitchen. Oh, well. She could see well enough to work. She began knitting, determined to get over the faint depression that had been plaguing her lately, the soft click and glide of the silver needles providing a familiar accompaniment to her thoughts. She needed to quit thinking about Rafe—about work—so much, and get her mind on other things, she decided. Things she enjoyed. Like reading. And knitting. She smiled wryly. Although making a sweater for her boss probably wasn't the best way to get him out of her mind. Especially since Rafe wouldn't like it if he knew how much work she'd put into it.

Rafe didn't like getting gifts, especially anything he considered too personal. Still, Lauren had decided to make him the sweater anyway. She'd made him a scarf last year, and he'd been okay with that. Besides, she enjoyed knitting and had no idea what else to get him for a Christmas gift.

So she'd indulged herself by choosing a merino lamb's wool in a deep, rich chocolate color to match his eyes. And she'd selected a fisherman stitch to challenge her skill. She held the garment up to judge her progress, pleased to notice that she only had a few inches left to complete. She should have it done in plenty of time for Christmas. He didn't have to know she'd made it, how many months it had taken her, she decided. Nor how expensive the yarn had been. She would just let him assume she'd bought it somewhere, and—

The doorbell chimed, interrupting her thoughts. Jay! she thought immediately, setting her work aside. Her neighbor had gotten in the habit of stopping by in the evenings to chat for a while, and Lauren enjoyed the visits, too. It made the long winter evenings pass more quickly.

Delighted at the prospect of company, Lauren opened the door with a smile of welcome on her face, shivering a little as the cold air rushed into the warm room.

Her smile slowly faded, and she pushed the door almost closed again, sheltering behind it. A man was standing on her unlit landing. His face was in profile, his shoulders braced against the sleet as he glanced back at something behind him. For a moment, she didn't recognize him.

But then he turned, and the light from the room behind her slanted across the hard angles of his face and lit up his intent eyes.

Lauren's heart skipped a beat, then picked up again at a faster pace. What was he doing here? He looked...

menacing somehow. But that was probably because of his evening beard. The dark stubble shaded his lean cheeks and chin, making him look like a gangster from an old black-and-white movie. The effect was heightened by his wet hair, which he'd slicked back off his forehead with a careless hand. Snowflakes glistened in the thick dark strands, and on the shoulders of his black overcoat.

For once his dark eyes looked serious—angry almost. But why would that be? Had something gone wrong at work?

"Rafe?" she said uncertainly.

Chapter Four

"Yeah, it's me." She looked surprised to see him, Rafe noticed. He could understand that. He was pretty surprised himself that he'd ended up on her doorstep this evening.

He stared down at her as she stood half-hidden by the door, her slight figure silhouetted by the light behind her. All day he'd told himself he wasn't going to come over here again—that he wasn't going to ask her a damn thing. Because even after seeing those baby bottles on her list, he still didn't believe Lauren was the woman Kane sought. That she'd deliberately get pregnant like that.

But then he'd realized that maybe it hadn't been deliberate. What if some guy—like this Jay character—had taken advantage of her? Gotten her into trouble? What if she'd accidentally gotten pregnant that way?

The more he'd thought about it, the more the evidence had added up. She'd been sick this morning—and had admitted she'd been ill all week. She'd also been awfully anxious not to let him into her apartment. Why, she'd practically raced to her bedroom to pull the door closed. He'd thought at the time she was embarrassed to have him see her clothes lying around, but maybe what she'd *really* been trying to prevent was him seeing someone else's clothes in there. Like a man's shirt. Or shoes. Or pants. That seemed a definite possibility.

But even more compelling was the feeling he'd been having lately; the one that until today he'd chalked up to his imagination. The feeling that Lauren was hiding something from him.

She wasn't as confiding as she'd been when they'd first started working together. More and more often, she'd have a shuttered, closed expression on her face when she looked at him. As if she had a secret she was determined not to share.

Not, Rafe reminded himself, that it was any of his business if Lauren didn't want to tell him about her personal life. She might be more naive than most women he knew, but she was still an adult, capable of making her own decisions—stupid though they might be.

Like unlocking her door without a moment's hesitation. That wasn't any of his business either, yet he couldn't help asking, "Don't you think you should check first to see who's out here before opening your door?"

"I usually do," Lauren said, tucking back a strand of hair that had fallen along her cheek. "But I was expecting someone."

"Jay, I suppose," he drawled.

She nodded. Even though Rafe had suspected as much, her ready agreement caused a spark of irritation to flare inside him. Not that it was any of his business who she hung out with on her time off, of course. Not at all.

"Is there something wrong? Do you want to come in?"

He glanced down at her again. She was staring up at

him with a puzzled, slightly worried expression. "Did you come over for anything special?" she added.

"I just stopped by to see how you were doing."

Her face lit up with shy pleasure, and she hugged the door a little closer. "I'm fine now. I don't feel sick at all anymore."

"That's great." Rafe shoved his hands into his pockets. "Glad to hear it."

But he didn't feel glad. If she had the flu, she should *still* have the flu, damn it! But morning sickness...

Not wanting to complete the thought, he pulled a folded sheet of paper from his pocket and held it out. "I also came to give you these notes from the meeting. Thought they'd help bring you up to speed on what's happening."

"Oh. Thank you." Some of Lauren's pleasure at his unexpected visit dimmed a bit. Of course he hadn't come *just* to see her; Rafe was a busy man. It made sense he'd also brought some work for her.

She accepted the paper, and when he made no move to leave, asked hesitantly, "Did you want to come in while I read this?"

No, he didn't want to come in. Rafe had decided that on the drive over. He'd hand her the notes—which were strictly company business—then leave. The storm was getting worse and driving would be a bitch as it was. He wanted to get on home.

"All right. Just for a moment." He stepped inside her tiny foyer.

"Let me take your coat."

He turned toward the living room as he shrugged it off. Nothing suspicious in there. Knitting needles hung from a brown sweater she'd tossed over a corner of the couch— a man's sweater judging by the size of the thing. The bundles of yarn lying next to it and on the floor were brown, too. Not pink, not blue, just plain old brown.

She folded his coat over a nearby chair, and clasped her hands together in front of her. "Would you like some tea?"

Tea? Rafe hated tea. "Okay."

He followed her into the kitchen. He leaned against the table, crossing his arms as he surreptitiously scanned her counters in search of a baby bottle. None were in sight. "Did you rest at all?" he asked idly.

"All afternoon." She opened a cupboard.

He glanced over to see if any bottles were on the shelves, and for the first time, really noticed what she was wearing. His eyebrows lifted in surprise.

Never before had he seen her dressed so casually. The gray sweat suit she had on was faded and worn, but it also looked soft and touchable. And he'd bet she wasn't wearing a bra under that baggy top—no, she wasn't, he noted, the suspicion confirmed as she stretched, reaching for a canister on the shelf. The movement caused the thin fleece of her top to press against her chest, revealing the small, tight peaks of her nipples.

"Pekoe? Or chamomile?"

"Huh?" His gaze jerked up to meet hers.

She tilted her head and wiggled the canister at him. "Which tea would you prefer?"

Neither. "Either."

She pulled out a tea bag, then turned toward the stove to get the kettle, her long hair swinging gently with the movement. It looked damp, as if she'd showered recently, and as she passed by him again, he smelled the crisp, soapy scent of her shampoo.

He watched her as she solemnly dipped the bag into the cup of hot water she'd poured. Her pale skin looked translucent, flawless—like that of a young child's. Not wearing her glasses made her look younger too. More vulnerable. Almost naked somehow.

A muscle tightened in his jaw. Was this how she dressed when that Jay guy came over? Didn't she know any better?

Clothes like that gave a man all sorts of ideas. Made him think how easy it would be for her to kick off those furry slippers as he carried her to bed. Or about cuddling her on his lap and pulling off those droopy pants. Hell, they were so loose they'd probably fall down on their own without much trouble. A man might be tempted to slide his cold hands beneath the soft gray fleece to stroke the warm, smooth skin of her flat stomach. Or higher yet to cup the slight curves of her breasts, to gently tease those enticing nipples into an even greater response.

Yeah, he'd bet that Jay character had thoughts just like that every time he looked at her, Rafe thought. His gaze swept over her again and his jaw clenched. The bastard.

Seeing the disapproval on Rafe's face, Lauren shifted uneasily. Tension radiated from his tall figure, making her oddly nervous. She wasn't sure exactly what was wrong— but one thing she did know: He sure didn't like the way she was dressed. The stern expression on his face as he looked her up and down made that more than clear. He was probably used to women greeting him at their doors wearing evening gowns or negligees. Or, at least, a decent blouse and pants. Certainly not in scruffy old sweats.

Feeling awkward, she set the tea bag aside, and handed him the cup. "Maybe I should change—"

"You're fine the way you are," he said, almost curtly as he accepted his tea. "I'm only going to stay a minute."

So, Rafe thought, hiding a grimace as he sipped the pale green liquid. For him—someone she'd known for almost three years—she felt she had to change. But for Jay...

None of your business, buddy, he reminded himself. *Not your business at all.*

He set his cup down on his saucer with a clatter. "Go ahead and check over the notes," he told her. "I should get on my way."

She nodded and began to unfold the paper he'd given her. Rafe's gaze lingered on the pale curve of her cheek and the fringe of her dark lashes as she stared down at the few lines he'd written there. Then she glanced up at him, a question in her blue-gray eyes as they met his. "There's not very much here."

"Yeah, I know." He'd been lucky to come up with that much, the meeting had been so short. He started talking, trying to come up with a reasonable explanation. "But I figured you'd want to be informed—"

Never mind that there wasn't too much yet to be informed about.

"—so I recorded—"

Made up.

"—our notes. Then, I decided you'd probably prefer to see them today, rather than waiting until Monday. So, I cruised over—"

Through a brewing blizzard.

"—to give them to you. That's the reason I'm here. The only reason—a *business* reason," he stressed. "And to find out how you are, of course," he added, suddenly remembering his previous inquiry.

Lauren blinked. She'd certainly never heard Rafe ramble on like that before. "Have you been drinking?"

"Of course not!" He glared at her. "Nothing but this da—this tea you just gave me. Why would you ask something like that?"

"No reason," Lauren said noncommittally. She glanced

down at the paper again. "I'm not sure what this says. Your handwriting is a little hard to read."

"You should talk," he muttered, not quite beneath his breath.

Lauren's head snapped up. "What did you say?"

Rafe stayed silent, content to give her his most skeptical expression.

"My writing is very readable," she said defensively.

"Yeah, right," he said in a bored tone.

Lauren stared at him. What was wrong with him? she wondered. He'd never complained about her handwriting before. "Is that all you wanted to give me?" she asked stiffly.

"Yeah. I'd better go."

She readily picked up his coat from the chair and handed it to him. He draped it over his his arm as he said, "Oh, yeah. You haven't forgotten you promised Kane you'd take care of the decorations for the company Christmas party, have you?"

"No, I haven't forgotten."

"He hasn't said anything, but I'm sure he's expecting you to help hostess this year, too."

"That'll be fun."

Still, he lingered without making any move to leave. "I guess you'll be pretty busy, especially since we have that business trip coming up in a couple of weeks."

"I probably will."

He fixed his intent, narrowed gaze on her as he added, "I hope the trip won't interfere with…your social life."

"It won't," she assured him, slightly surprised by the remark and the edge of sarcasm in his voice. Since when did Rafe care about her social life?

But it seemed Rafe cared about a lot of things she didn't suspect. "How's Jay?" he suddenly demanded.

"Jay's fine," Lauren answered, bewildered by the change of topic.

"I don't see how you have time to visit with anyone," he growled, "when we've been so busy at work."

Ah, *now* she understood. Lauren's annoyance eased. Rafe must be acting so strangely because he was tired. He'd admitted this morning to feeling a little stressed. He'd probably worked too hard today—especially without her there to help him.

The thought that he needed her made her feel soft inside. "Yes, we have been busy," she agreed. "You'd better get home and rest."

Rafe stared at the slight smile on her lips, the warm light in her eyes and set his back teeth. Okay, fine. So she wasn't going to tell him...in fact, she was kicking him out of her house. Well, that was great, because he didn't want to know.

He swung around toward the door. He wasn't going to get involved; he didn't need this hassle. It wasn't any of his business, and he really didn't care.

He had his hand on the doorknob when something registered—something he'd glimpsed from the corner of his eye. He glanced back for a second look.

Beady black eyes met his. What he'd taken to be a bundle of yarn was actually a bear. A stuffed, furry brown bear almost hidden by the sweater she'd been working on.

That was it. The final straw. The bear that broke the camel's back.

He tossed his coat over the chair again. He swung around to face her. "Okay, Lauren, you might as well tell me everything. I know what you've been trying to hide."

Chapter Five

Lauren stared at him. She felt the blood drain from her cheeks. "You do?" Her stomach clenched. She wrapped her arms around her waist, trying to ease the odd sensation.

His gaze dropped to her stomach, covered protectively by her crossed arms, and his expression hardened. He nodded curtly. "It wasn't hard to figure out, once I'd put all the facts together."

A painful flush rose, burning up her neck to her face. "It wasn't?"

"No."

How humiliating. Lauren stared miserably down at her slippers, not knowing what to say, wishing he would just leave. But it seemed Rafe still wasn't through.

He turned and strode toward the couch where her knitting lay abandoned. His voice emerged on a low growl as he added, "Especially after I saw this damned—"

Sweater, Lauren thought, shutting her eyes in despair.

"Bear!"

Lauren's eyes popped open—just in time to see Rafe

pounce on poor Teddy. He snatched it up, and gave the little stuffed creature a savage shake.

Lauren's mouth dropped open—then snapped shut. "What are you doing?" she asked, thrown off balance by his strange actions. And as his words registered, "And what does that have to do with anything?"

Rafe was glaring down at Teddy, but he spared her a glance to say, "C'mon, Lauren. I know who this bear is for."

Lauren frowned in confusion. "That's my bear. I bought it over a year ago."

"You did?" His eyebrows lifted in surprise. "Why did you do that?"

"Because I like them, of course. Everyone likes teddy bears."

Everyone, apparently, except Rafe. He shook Teddy at her as he demanded, "So you didn't buy it for the baby?"

"What baby?"

"Your baby!" he roared. "The one we've been talking about."

Rafe paused—she looked completely bewildered. Tossing the bear back on the couch, he put his hands on his hips, determined to get to the bottom of things. "Damn it, Lauren, are you pregnant—or aren't you?"

She gasped. "Of course I'm not pregnant!"

"You're not?"

"No. Is *that* what you thought?" Relief flickered across her face. "Whatever made you think I was going to have a baby?"

"You were sick this morning—and then you felt better." Rafe raked a hand through his hair as she just stared at him, obviously waiting for him to continue. "And then there was the bear—and—" he shoved his hand into his pocket and pulled out another paper "—and *this!*"

He thrust the crumpled sheet at her. Lauren accepted it gingerly. It looked as if it had been crushed by his fist it was so wrinkled and wadded up. She spread it open and glanced down. Heat rose in her cheeks again as she recognized the list she'd made in his office that morning. "Oh. I'd forgotten about this."

"I thought you had," Rafe said in grim triumph. He jabbed at one of the items with his finger. "Let's hear you explain *this* away, if you can."

Lauren's face burned hotter, but she decided to give it a shot. "Well, as you probably figured out, the devil represents you. And I drew the tail around to the front like that because—"

"Not that!" Rafe snatched the paper away. "I meant item number three. The one about the baby bottles!"

"Baby? —Oh." The puzzled crease in her brow smoothed out as realization dawned. "Those are for the women's shelter. The director asked if I would pick some up."

"Oh."

"Yes, oh." Lauren repeated, her relief turning to amusement at the blank look on his face. That seemed to blow a little steam out of his engine.

Rafe frowned down at the paper. That made sense; so much sense he didn't know why he hadn't seen it for himself. He tried to find an excuse for his misunderstanding. "If the bottles were for the shelter, then why didn't you put them down after the first item where you mentioned it?" he demanded.

Lauren shrugged. "I don't know. My mind was jumping around, I guess. But obviously not as much as yours has been. Why on earth would a little thing like that make you think I'm going to have a baby?"

The dry tone of her voice, the amusement in her eyes,

made Rafe feel foolish. "That wasn't the only reason," he defended himself. "Kane was the one who started it off, saying something that sounded as if you—as if he—as if you and he might have...." He trailed off, suddenly realizing that Kane might not want his sperm problem spread all over the firm.

Lauren's eyes had gone wide again. "Kane Haley said he and I were lovers?"

"No, of course not," Rafe said. "That's ridiculous..."

Lauren stiffened. Ridiculous?

"...Although, I have to admit, for a second I had that crazy idea, too." He shook his head. "But I know Kane would never fool around with one of his employees, and besides, you're not..." He paused. "Well, I mean you aren't..."

She pressed her lips together. "I'm not what?"

"The, ah, kind of woman he...dates."

Hurt bloomed in Lauren's chest, replacing the relief that she'd been feeling. "So what you're saying is that Kane Haley would never be interested in a woman like me," she repeated, each word stabbing her a little.

Rafe gave her a sharp glance. Did she want Haley's attention? Because it sure sounded that way from her tone.

And he didn't like the thought, not at all. Lauren and Kane? No way. She was much too young for Haley. Rafe was trying to come up with a subtle way to ask her if she was interested in the man when she got in first with a question of her own.

"So, if you figured out Kane Haley hadn't gotten me pregnant, then who was supposed to have done the dastardly deed?"

Jay Leonardo leaped to the forefront of Rafe's mind, but he kept his mouth shut. If Lauren hadn't considered Leonardo as a lover, then why put the idea in her head? Rafe didn't care for the man—never had, and never would. Never mind that he'd never met him. He just had a feeling that Leonardo—like Kane—would be bad news for Lauren.

"Oh, I don't know," he said vaguely, not wanting to delve into the subject too deeply. "Accidents happen. All it takes is one careless night and..."

Lauren stared at him as his voice trailed off again. After working with her for three years, didn't he know her any better? Didn't he realize she would never do something like that? Or how insulting it was for him to even suggest it? Did he even care?

No, of course not. Rafe Mitchell didn't really care how she felt, not at all. "So you think I'm the kind of woman who has one-night stands?"

Rafe's head whipped up at her dangerously quiet tone. His gaze locked with hers. "Hell, no," he said, backpedaling rapidly, amazed at how upset—even angry—she suddenly looked. Lauren never got angry. Oh, she got incensed at times over the state of the economy or the environment—and world hunger *really* got her going—but she never lost her temper. At least not with him.

He was used to teasing her, making her laugh—riling her up a little, sure—but not to the point where she looked liked she was ready to come after him.

"I don't think that at all. But you don't know how men are, how they think, and I do," he explained in an effort to placate her. "I just figured that since you're kind of naive, and you haven't dated much—some jerk might have taken advantage of that."

Too bad Lauren didn't look placated. Her eyes narrowed—as if she was sighting down a rifle at him. A bad sign. She unclenched her hands—a good sign—but then crossed her arms over her breasts. Not so good.

"I see," she said. "So what you *really* think is the only reason a man would date me is for sex."

"I don't think that!"

"So, I'm *not* the kind of woman men want to have sex with?"

"Of course not—"

"How dare you!"

"I mean, yes—no. Hell, I don't know what I mean anymore." Rafe raked his hand through his hair.

"At least you admit you don't know what you're talking about," she concluded in a silky, condescending voice.

Rafe wasn't used to arguing with Lauren, and he certainly wasn't accustomed to seeing disdain in her gentle eyes, hearing sarcasm in her soft voice when she spoke to him. "What's wrong with you tonight?" he demanded.

"What's wrong with *me?*" Her eyes blazed with hurt and anger. "You come over here, on a day when I've been sick, call me naive and insult me in ten different ways—sticking your nose into something that is none of your business—and you have the gall to ask *me* what's wrong?"

Her pale face was bleak and set. She picked up his coat and held it out to him. "I think you'd better go."

Rafe stared at her, as amazed as if a kitten had suddenly turned into a tiger. "But, Lauren..."

She thrust his coat into his arms, refusing even to look at him again. She pulled the door open wide, letting the freezing cold blow in, showing him the way out. "Just go!"

So, with a stifled oath, Rafe left.

Chapter Six

Lauren shut the door and locked it. Then she walked into her living room and sank down onto the couch.

She hugged herself, fighting back the tears burning in her eyes, refusing to let them fall. No way was she going to break down now. She'd had plenty of practice controlling her emotions; doing so had become almost second nature to her over the past two years.

Ever since the day she'd fallen in love with Rafe.

Even at the time she'd known it was stupid to let it happen. Rafe wasn't the kind of man she'd ever dreamed of loving someday. She'd thought she'd choose somebody like her father—a quiet, handsome man, who hadn't been ambitious in the least, but whose life had revolved around his wife and little daughter.

Rafe wasn't exceptionally handsome. Not really. His face was all planes and angles, his nose had a slight bump on the bridge from when he'd boxed in the marines. His mouth was too wide, his lips too thin and his eyes too often held a cynical expression that made him seem far older than his years.

And he was ambitious; relentlessly so. The takeovers he orchestrated were ruthless and swift, usually completed before the other company quite knew what was happening. He was perfect for the position he held at Kane Haley, Inc.—but not as the kind of man to dream about. Lauren had been aware of that from the moment she'd met him.

But then Rafe had shown up at her door with a tree her very first Christmas in the city. Her very first Christmas alone. She'd looked into his teasing brown eyes, seen that crooked smile on his face as he pushed his way into her home with that pine, and she'd fallen in love for the first time in her life.

And once she'd started sliding down that slippery slope, it had been impossible to stop. All day she'd just kept falling—swept away by the intent expression on his lean face as he'd hung tinsel on the tree, one silver strand at a time; charmed by the care with which he handled the antique glass ornaments she'd inherited from her mom. Comforted by the way he hugged her to his hard, warm chest when grief had briefly overcome her and a few tears had escaped to trail slowly down her cheeks.

He'd let her cry—then teased her into laughing again. When he discovered she didn't have a topper for the tree, he'd created one himself out of a pink paper cup. He'd made coffee so strong her hair almost stood on end, and sugar cookies so underbaked they were practically still dough. The day had been filled with the scent of pine, twinkling lights, the sound of laughter and the soft silence of snowflakes falling outside the window; with the warmth of the fire burning cheerily in the hearth and the taste of hot chocolate and peppermint. Memories of Christmas— and of Rafe.

When the day was over and he'd left, Lauren had told herself that she only imagined that he'd taken her heart with him. A combination of the holidays and emotions. She'd worked to bury her feelings deep inside, and for months at a time, she managed to pretend he was just her boss. A great guy to work for. A friend.

But every day lately it seemed to be getting harder to hide her feelings. Her stomach would twist in knots at an unexpected smile or a touch of his hand. She worried constantly about giving herself away; had even thought tonight that he'd guessed her secret. Thank goodness, he hadn't. She knew Rafe wasn't interested in her that way. Although, until their argument, she hadn't realized he thought she had no sexual appeal for any man at all.

She swallowed hard, hugging herself tighter—then stiffened as a knock sounded at the door. Pain shot through her. *Oh, please, couldn't he just go away?* She couldn't face Rafe again tonight.

But a second later, a feminine voice called, "Lauren? Are you all right?" and she realized in relief it wasn't Rafe coming back to torment her unknowingly. It was Jay.

Usually Lauren loved having her neighbor stop by to visit. She'd first met her at the women's shelter where Jay, a cosmetologist, had been demonstrating makeup techniques to help some of the women prepare for job interviews. The two had quickly become firm friends—so much so, that when the apartment next door had become vacant a month ago, Lauren had told Jay who'd immediately snapped it up.

Although Jay's quirky outlook on life always made her fun to be around, Lauren wasn't up to having fun tonight. Yet, when her friend called her name again with increasing concern in her voice, Lauren knew she couldn't just ignore her. With a sigh, she went and opened the door.

Jay took one look at her face, then gently brushed her aside and marched in. Her long black hair flowed down her back like a cape, and she carried her huge tote bag slung over one slim shoulder as she followed Lauren to the couch.

Lauren sat down, gesturing to Jay to do the same. Jay shed her bag, her amber coat and orange silk scarf onto the floor, then perched next to her.

"Okay, what's going on here? Who was that man and why did he make you cry?" Jay demanded.

"I'm not crying." Lauren defiantly swallowed the lump in her throat. "That was just my boss—Rafe."

"Did he fire you?" Jay rummaged in her bag and pulled out a package of tissues.

"No, of course—"

"Hit on you then?" Jay interrupted. Without waiting for an answer, she added grimly, "I just knew he was going to do that someday."

Lauren accepted the tissue Jay held out. "Well, he didn't." A small, bitter laugh escaped her. "In fact, you couldn't be more wrong. If anything he did the opposite."

Jay's perfectly plucked dark eyebrows arched higher. "He *refused* to go to bed with you?"

"Yes—well, no." Lauren blew her nose. "That is, the subject didn't come up—but if it had, he would have."

"So why did he come here?"

"Because he thought I was pregnant."

Jay gasped, pressing a startled hand against her plump bosom. "With his baby?"

"No! Of course not."

"He thought it was someone else's?"

"Oh, for heaven's sake, I'm not pregnant," Lauren said in exasperation. "He just thinks I'm naive and I don't know anything about men, and that something might have happened. He sounded as if—as if the only reason a man would ever go out with me, was if he was desperate for sex. *Very* desperate.''

Jay had no trouble at all deciphering the main point of that confusing statement. "That jerk!"

"Oh, he didn't intend to hurt me," Lauren admitted. "Rafe's not like that. In fact, I'm almost positive he feels a certain amount of—of affection for me. He's always teasing me, the way he would a little sister. I'm the one who deluded myself into thinking he'd ever consider me more than that.''

"And why shouldn't he? You're a wonderful woman."

Lauren gave her friend's hand an impulsive squeeze of thanks, but shook her head, smiling wryly. "I certainly can't compete with the women he goes out with. They're stunning—as well as sophisticated. Never mind having figures like—like Victoria's Secret models.''

"Big breasts, huh?" Jay said bluntly. She ignored Lauren's remarks about the women's attractiveness to ask the question that interested her more. "What do you mean *women?* As in plural? What is this guy? Some kind of player?''

"No. Not exactly. At least—I know he's honest with the women he dates. He lets them know he doesn't believe in love.''

"But I bet every one of them thinks she'll be the one to change his mind," Jay said shrewdly.

"Probably," Lauren agreed dispiritedly. How could she doubt it? Hadn't she secretly had the same hope? And he hadn't even been dating her.

"He's a player, all right," Jay was saying, conviction in her voice. "And smart enough to know there's safety in numbers. Well, then forget about the man. He doesn't deserve a woman like you."

A wave of misery welled up in Lauren. "No," she agreed. "He deserves someone who's sophisticated and beautiful. The kind of woman he enjoys going around with."

"Lauren Connor, you stop that right now," Jay scolded, her ebony eyes flashing. "You're beautiful—"

"Oh, sure..."

"Yes, you are. But until you get one person to believe it, no one else will."

Lauren blew her nose again, thinking that over. "You mean Rafe?" she asked hesitantly, glancing at her friend over the top of her tissue.

"Goodness, no, I don't mean Rafe! Didn't I just tell you to forget the man? I mean you!"

"Me? But I'm *not* beautiful." Lauren didn't want to make Jay angry, but they needed to face reality here.

But Jay appeared unwilling to do that. "Oh?" she demanded. "What makes you say that?"

"Because I'm so—so unnoticeable."

Jay gave her clothes a disparaging glance. "So quit wearing clothes that resemble a mud puddle. Get something with color, something that highlights your wonderful skin tone. And tighter, more form-fitting to show off your figure. Most women would just about die to be as slender as you are."

"But not to be built like me."

Jay rolled her eyes. "Oh, please. Just because your breasts aren't huge—"

"That's an understatement."

"—doesn't mean your figure is bad. Your legs are long and slim, your waist is slender, your stomach is flat. You've been blessed, girl." She studied Lauren's face, saying earnestly, "Don't you see? The way you feel about yourself affects the way you think and dress and react to other people—and how they react to you. You shouldn't want to be someone else—not even the kind of woman you think some man might want. You have to be the kind of woman *you* want to be.''

Lauren knew all that, of course. It was the same talk she'd heard Jay give a dozen times at the shelter. But she'd never applied it to herself—had never even considered it. "I *am* the kind of woman I want to be," she protested.

"Are you?" Jay demanded. "I don't think you think about yourself much at all. Do you like gray?" she asked, looking pointedly at Lauren's sweat suit.

"No, not particularly…"

"And wearing your hair long?"

Lauren fingered the strands hanging over her shoulders. "No, not especially. It's just easier—"

"Forget easy. Do you like the way it *looks?*"

"No," Lauren said—and realized she'd been tired of her hairstyle for ages. "I think it would look better short. But I'm always so busy. With work, and helping at the shelter and…" Her voice trailed off.

"And sitting at home, dreaming about this Rafe." Jay's voice was stern, but the expression in her eyes was gentle as she said, "You have to stop it, Lauren. If you don't, he's bound to discover how you feel sometime. And then, you may end up just being one of Rafe's women. Do you really want that?"

No, she didn't want that. As much as she hurt now, she knew that to belong to Rafe however briefly and then have him move on would hurt a thousand times more. "So how do I fight it?"

"You have to quit focusing on the man so much, quit thinking about him all the time, and start going after the kind of man you do want."

"Visualization," Lauren said automatically. "Athletes

do it. We use it all the time at work. You visualize what you want, then imagine it happening." Her mouth turned down wryly. "Rafe is really good at it."

"Well, you can learn to be good at it, too," Jay said stoutly.

Lauren wasn't sure about that, but she did know one thing. She couldn't go on like this, pining after a man who didn't want her. Wasting her life sitting around hoping that Rafe would fall in love with her—and only her—someday. He'd never fallen in love with any of the extraordinary women he dated, so why had she imagined he'd fall in love with her? Thinking he'd ever return her regard had been sheer make-believe on her part.

Especially since she now knew what he really thought of her. That she wasn't beautiful or intelligent enough to interest a man like Kane Haley—or a man like Rafe Mitchell. That she was the kind of woman who was so desperate for male attention, she'd consider having a one-night stand.

Hurt pride stiffened her spine. Jay was right. She needed to change her way of thinking. Change herself. Go after what she wanted. Find a man who wanted the same things in life that she did. A home. A family. And most of all, love.

"You're right—about Rafe, about everything," she told Jay, then glanced down at her sweat suit with a grimace, remembering Rafe's expression when he'd seen her in it. "And there's no better place to start than with a new wardrobe."

Jay clapped her hands together. "Atta girl! You and I have some shopping and some cutting and some pampering to do this weekend."

Energized by the mere thought, Jay rose to her feet and discovered she'd been sitting on something. "Oh, goodness—what's this?" she asked, picking up the sweater

Lauren had been knitting. She held it up—then glanced silently at Lauren.

But Lauren didn't meet her eyes; her gaze was fixed on the garment in Jay's hands. Lauren thought again how well the rich chocolate color would become Rafe. How warm it would keep him during the cold Chicago winters.

She reached out and took the sweater from Jay. Stroking the soft, thick wool, she thought of the hours, the weeks, the months she'd worked on it.

"Are you still going to give it to him?" Jay asked quietly.

Lauren shook her head. "No," she said, calmly. "I'm not."

She slipped her needles out of their loops and tugged at the strands of wool. Steadily, she began unraveling her stitches, winding the yarn back into a ball.

She glanced at her friend and forced a smile. "So, while I do this, why don't you show me what you've got in that bag of tricks of yours?"

Chapter Seven

Rafe arrived at work at a ridiculously early hour on Monday morning. He hadn't slept well the night before—or all weekend, in fact.

As a kid, he'd often had a hard time sleeping. He'd lie awake in bed for hours, monitoring the sounds made by the other people in the latest foster home he'd been dumped in. At times he'd been wise to be wary. At others, the people had turned out to be okay. It didn't matter. He couldn't relax with strangers so near.

As he grew older, tougher and wiser, it wasn't wariness that plagued him at night but restlessness. He'd slip out into the darkness and roam the streets, trying to ease some of his intense physical energy with a pickup game of basketball. Or with a willing girl who had energy to burn, too.

These days, he used the dark, sleepless hours to work on business projects. He'd found that to be as good a remedy as any—and definitely beneficial to his career. Yeah, he'd never been one to sleep much, Rafe thought. But he couldn't remember the last time guilt had kept him awake.

Remorse—unfamiliar and uncomfortable—surged through him. He pushed aside the report he'd been writing and leaned back in his chair. All weekend he'd thought about Lauren, wondered if he should call and try to apologize once again for inadvertently insulting her. But finally he'd reached the conclusion he should give her some time alone to get over the hurt he'd inflicted. He'd decided to make his apology when she came into work. On neutral ground, so to speak.

Restlessly, he checked his watch. She should be arriving soon. He hoped she wasn't still upset; he hadn't meant to make her feel bad. As he'd told Kane, Lauren was sweet—but way too sensitive, he decided. After she forgave him, he'd mention—tactfully, of course—that she should work on that a bit.

He reached for his report again to get back to work himself and knocked his gold pen to the floor. He bent to pick it up and finally located it under his desk. He stretched to grab it…and paused.

Framed in the opening beneath his desk, he could see a pair of legs approaching—long, shapely feminine legs that tapered down to slender ankles and small feet clad in knock-'em-dead high heels.

Curious to view the rest of the package, he jerked up—and banged his head on the edge of his desk.

Stars sparkled. He winced, his eyes squeezing shut. "Damn!" he muttered, rubbing at the sore spot.

"Are you all right?" a soft voice asked.

"Yeah, I'm—Lauren?"

"Um-hmm."

Rafe opened his eyes—and felt his jaw drop. He snapped it shut, but continued to stare at the woman standing before him. Exactly how hard had he whacked his head anyway? he wondered.

"Lauren?" he repeated—because he could hardly believe it. She looked so—so un-Laurenlike. "What did you do to yourself?"

"I made a few changes."

She certainly had. His gaze moved over her, cataloging those changes, as she walked over to her chair. The change from the drab, loose tops she usually wore to a pink sweater that clung to her slender figure, revealing the high, delicate curves of her breasts. The black wool skirt that hugged her slim hips and hiked up above her knees as she sat down and crossed her legs. Not to mention those killer black shoes with the heels high enough to give her a nosebleed from the change in altitude.

And the differences didn't stop there.

"You're not wearing your glasses," he said, as if she didn't know.

She nodded, clasping her hands on the papers and pad she was holding on her lap. "I have on contacts. I've had them for a while now, but I've never worn them to work because they make my eyes water so much. But Jay thinks I look better without my glasses, so I'm trying to get used to them."

Jay again—and damn it, Jay was right, Rafe thought. Without the dark frames overpowering her small face, her eyes looked bigger and brighter—maybe because they were watering, as she'd said. But their blue-gray color looked different, too. Smokier, somehow, and edged by lashes that were surprisingly long and dark and thick.

"I suppose Jay suggested the haircut, too," he said dryly.

He watched her hair swing gently as she nodded. Instead of hanging straight down, her hair now curved under her chin. Shiny and thick, with unexpected streaks of honey gleaming among the rich brown strands, it had a tousled look. As if she'd run her fingers through it as she climbed out of bed.

The style definitely suited her, he admitted grudgingly, reluctant to give Jay any credit. Her cheekbones appeared more pronounced. The clean, delicate line of her jaw was revealed, and her mouth.... Rafe's gaze lingered on her mouth. Her new lipstick—the same shade as a rich red wine—made her mouth look fuller, poutier. Moist and soft. Enticingly kissable.

With an effort, he looked away from her lips. Yeah, she'd changed all right. The only familiar thing about her was the serious, resolute expression she was wearing. She seemed to have her game face on.

She pressed her lips together. "Rafe—"

"Yeah?" He shifted restlessly, letting his gaze run over her again. Altogether, she looked more polished, more together and definitely more sophisticated. Yet contradictorily, she also looked more rumpled somehow. Looser. Softer. Sexier. The kind of woman he could imagine sprawled across his bed, her creamy skin flushed with the afterglow of— *Whoa there, buddy. This is Lauren you're fantasizing about here. Not some sexy babe.*

"I'd like to request a transfer."

Rafe jerked, startled back to reality by the determined note in Lauren's voice. "Did you say transfer?"

She sat stiffly in her chair. "Yes. I want to spread my wings a bit. Gain experience in a few other departments."

And get away from you, he supplied silently, feeling an unexpected pang of hurt at the thought.

Hell, she couldn't really mean it. She was just angry about what he'd said. "Lauren, if this is about the other night—"

"It isn't," she insisted, interrupting his apology. "My request has nothing to do with that at all."

He didn't believe her. But he knew she wouldn't admit the truth. He considered her request a moment, trying to decide on the best way to handle it. She was obviously braced for a battle. The rose-pink color of her sweater was echoed in her cheeks, and even the soft material couldn't disguise the proud, straight set of her shoulders.

He glanced at her hands. Sure enough, her slim fingers were gripping her notepad so tightly that her knuckles had turned white.

So, she expected a fight, did she? Then he wasn't going to give her one. "Okay," he said, "you can have a transfer..."

Her gaze flew up to meet his. Surprise was in her wet blue eyes. But before she could say anything, he added, "...but not until the Bartlett merger goes through. I don't want to have to train another secretary in the middle of a deal as important as this one."

A small crease appeared between her brows. She bit her lip, thinking that over, while Rafe watched her from beneath drooping eyelids, thinking how white—and sharp—her small teeth looked against the rich burgundy color of her mouth.

"How much longer do you think this merger will take?" she finally asked.

He shrugged. "I hope to wind it up on our trip to Hillsboro."

She hesitated, studying his unrevealing expression. "All right," she said reluctantly. Then lifting her chin, she added in the distant tone she'd used the other night, "But I'd appreciate it if you'd begin processing my request right away."

He'd appreciate it if she'd quit being so sensitive, Rafe

thought, feeling a prickle of annoyance. What he'd done had been rude—and totally unforgivable. But it was time to forget about it and get back to normal. "And I think that—"

He broke off as a quick knock sounded on his open door. He glanced in that direction. Brandon Levy, a college kid who worked in the mail room in the mornings while he finished up his business degree at night, strode in without waiting for an invitation.

Brandon always moved quickly, if awkwardly, like a gangly giraffe. He was halfway across the room in less than two seconds, his gaze fixed on the envelopes in his hands. "Sorry to interrupt," he said, looking up in time to catch Rafe's frowning glance. "But these letters were marked Urgent so I thought I'd better bring them up right away."

"I'll take them," Lauren offered, holding out her hand.

"Okay," Brandon turned her way, shuffling through the envelopes. "I have a few here for Maggie as well, so I'll just—" He lifted his head—and froze.

Rafe watched as the kid just stood there—like a lovesick pup—staring at Lauren with a look of amazement on his face, his arm extended to hand her the envelopes.

Then Lauren smiled, and leaned forward to take them, breaking the spell. Brandon came back to life with a start, almost leaping the two feet remaining to place them in her hands. "Ah, here you go."

"Thank you, Brandon," she replied.

A wave of color rose up Brandon's face, all the way past his tanned forehead to his blond, spiked hair. "You're welcome, Lauren," he replied, his husky young voice lingering on her name.

Then, as she reached for the opener on Rafe's desk,

Brandon leaped again, grabbing that up, too. He handed it to her—earning yet another grateful smile.

"Thank you again," Lauren said.

"You're welcome again," Brandon replied, and to Rafe's disgust, a big goofy grin spread across the boy's face, as if he thought he'd said something clever.

Rafe resisted the urge to throw the kid out of his office. Lauren wouldn't like that, he knew without a doubt. But when a full ten seconds passed, and the kid still hadn't moved, Rafe decided to prod him along. "You said you had some mail for Maggie, too?"

"Oh, yeah. Yeah, I did," Brandon said with regret in his voice. Rafe watched him slowly make his way to the door. The kid was practically walking backward in an effort to keep his eyes fixed on Lauren as long as possible. Rafe wasn't surprised at all when he backed into the basketball trash can, still centered on the carpet. Brandon stumbled—recovered his balance—and with another tide of red rising on his face, finally made it out of the room.

Rafe shook his head in disbelief. He leaned back in his chair, and glanced at Lauren, expecting her to share his amusement. "Can you believe it?"

"Believe what?" she parroted back, without looking up from the envelopes she was slitting open.

"Brandon," Rafe said impatiently. "Didn't you notice the way he acted? He was all over you."

That caught her attention. She slowly looked up, her eyebrows rising beneath the new, wispy fringe of golden-brown hair on her forehead. "Hardly. He just handed me some envelopes and a letter opener."

"And practically drooled all over you as he did it."

"Oh, please." She returned her attention to the envelopes.

With any other woman, Rafe would have thought she

was pretending not to notice Brandon's infatuation. But Lauren simply hadn't seen it. He should just let it go, Rafe knew, but he couldn't help asking one more question. "How long has that kid been calling you Lauren anyway?"

"For as long as he's been working here."

Rafe frowned. "That seems kind of overly friendly, almost disrespectful, don't you think?"

Lauren stared at him again. "You have to be joking," she said, dryly. "That 'kid' is a mere four years younger than I am. There's twice that difference between your age and mine. Is this a not-so-subtle hint that you'd like me to call you Mr. Mitchell? That *I've* been overly friendly?"

"Hell, no," Rafe said hastily. That was the last thing he'd accuse her of this morning. Besides, the situations weren't similar at all—and she knew it. Brandon was a kid and she was a woman. Rafe, on the other hand, was a man and she was...well, still a woman.

She was watching him expectantly—as if waiting for him to debate the issue—but Rafe decided to let the matter drop. He didn't want to get sidetracked into another ridiculous argument like the one they'd had the other night— especially another argument that he suspected he wouldn't win. What he intended to do was settle the one they'd had.

"Lauren, about the other night—" He gave her a rueful smile. "I'm sorry. I never intended to say what I did."

To his surprise, she smiled back. "That's okay. Forget about it," she said, almost cheerfully, "Actually, you did me a favor."

"I did?"

She nodded. "I thought over what you said, and I decided you were right."

That should have been a good thing, yet Rafe suddenly

felt wary—as if he were in the marines again, picking his way through a field full of land mines. "Right about what?" he asked cautiously.

"What you're always telling me. That I need to develop some backbone. Set goals, get out more. That I should learn to fight for what I want."

Rafe relaxed again, leaning back in his chair. He gave her an approving nod, pleased that she was finally taking his advice. "Good. Glad to hear it. So what is it that you decided you want?"

"A man."

"What!" Rafe straightened so abruptly, his chair almost fell over. "What did you say?"

"I said a man, Rafe. Remember? Those creatures you know everything about." She gathered up her papers, preparing to depart.

Rafe's mouth tightened. "I suppose this is another suggestion made by your new friend Jay. And I suppose he intends to be the man in question."

She stared at him a moment, then her gaze shifted as she stood up. "No, I don't think so. Jay and I are—just friends."

Rafe could see the amusement on her face, and his annoyance increased. Okay—now he got it. She was jerking him around, pulling his leg. He said dryly, "I thought you were insulted the other night, when I inadvertently implied you might have had a one-night stand."

"I was insulted—I'm still insulted—by such a suggestion, inadvertent or not." Turning her head, she met his eyes steadily. "Everyone isn't like you, Rafe, only capable of brief affairs. I'm looking for a serious relationship. One that will lead to marriage."

"Marriage!"

She nodded, amusement—and an odd kind of sadness—

still in her eyes. "Yes. *Mar-riage,*" she said, enunciating each syllable as if teaching him a foreign word. She started walking to the door.

Now he *knew* she was joking. "C'mon, Lauren. That's ridiculous," he said, letting his exasperation show in his voice. "You can't decide to get married, just like that, and go out and find a man. That's not how it happens."

Until that moment, Lauren might have agreed. She'd gone along with Jay's makeover plan more to take her mind off Rafe, than because she thought it might work. She knew she was still the same person despite the new dress and makeup.

But to hear him dismiss her goal with such scorn, with such absolute certainty in his voice, aroused her determination as nothing else could have done.

"You wanna bet?" she asked quietly. Then walked out, shutting the door behind her.

Rafe gritted his teeth, resisting the urge to go after her. She was getting good at that, he thought grimly. Good at shutting a door between them before he could talk some sense into her.

His hands clenched on the arms of his chair. He couldn't believe that she'd take his sound, practical business advice and twist it around to suit such an absurd goal as marriage. Marriage wasn't something a person pursued. It was something that happened when a person didn't expect it—like a car accident.

Lauren couldn't want that. No sane person did. Did she really think she wanted to tie herself down to one person? To go home every night to talk, to sleep—to make *love*—with someone like this Jay Leonardo character? Hell, no. The mere thought of Lauren with somebody like Leonardo made Rafe want to puke.

In fact, Lauren didn't need to be going out at all, he

decided. She was only twenty-four, for God's sake. Much too young to be running around loose. Memories of himself at twenty-four flitted though his mind, but he pushed the thoughts away. He'd been in the marines, damn it. And he was a man. Lauren was...well, Lauren.

And that summed it up in a nutshell. Lauren was too young, too sweet—too damned innocent—to know what she was saying. She didn't need a man. She had a boss. Him.

And he intended to remain her boss. He picked up the transfer request she'd left on his desk. They worked well together. She didn't really want to transfer—she just thought she did because he'd gotten her upset. Things were fine the way they were. Or at least, the way they had been before Kane Haley had come to his office and started this whole mess. Damn Kane, anyway, with his crazy pregnancy problems.

If it hadn't been for Haley, Lauren wouldn't be off on this wild crusade to find a man. A crusade Rafe totally disapproved of. This was a business corporation—not some damn dating agency. He didn't need a bunch of infatuated males—like Brandon—stumbling around in his office, causing complications. Lauren didn't need them either.

This was simply some kind of female funk she'd fallen into. A person didn't change so completely, just overnight. She'd get tired of her quest—revert back to her normal self soon. He was sure of it.

But until she did, he would simply have to watch out for her. Make sure she didn't get into any trouble with her "new look." Prevent any problems from arising.

He could do that. No sweat. He was good at handling problems. Crumpling up her transfer request, he tossed it in the can.

Yeah, he was damn good.

Chapter Eight

A full week passed before Lauren realized her plan was being sabotaged. She might not have realized it at all if she hadn't run into Julia Parker in the women's restroom one day after lunch.

"I love your new hairstyle," Julia told Lauren, who was standing in front of the mirror, as she strode past. "And that outfit looks great on you."

"Thanks." Brush in hand, Lauren watched the other woman disappear into one of the stalls, then glanced back at her own image. She'd teamed her black boots with her emerald-green dress today and was pleased by the compliment. Especially since it came from Julia. Fashion, Jay had informed her, was something that came and went, while style was a personal statement a person made about themselves with their clothes. Julia definitely had style.

Even six months pregnant, the blonde always looked chic yet businesslike—and still very slender—in the clothes she wore to work. Earning a compliment from her reassured Lauren that her new look was a definite improvement.

And she needed the reassurance. She'd never felt so conspicuous in her life as she had this past week. She felt as though everyone was looking at her. Until she'd gotten rid of them she hadn't realized how she'd used her long hair, loose clothes and glasses as a barrier—or maybe camouflage—to protect her from the possible attention of men.

Not that she needed to worry. So far, not one man had noticed the change—except for Rafe, of course, that day she'd asked for a transfer. And mentioning that she wasn't wearing her glasses had hardly been much of a compliment.

Since then, he'd practically ignored her for the most part. In fact, he often looked grim when she wore a new outfit to work. Sometimes he'd even glance away, as if he couldn't bear to look at her.

It hurt, but Lauren tried to ignore his reaction. Knowing how he felt made getting over him that much easier, she'd told herself bracingly. And it would be easier still, when her transfer came through and she was no longer with him all day long, five days a week.

Still, it had been hard to request a transfer. She enjoyed her job, enjoyed working with Rafe. But she'd decided she'd overcome her unhealthy addiction to him more quickly by transferring to another department. Leaving the firm would probably be even better, but she doubted she could match the money she was earning at Kane Haley, Inc., and she didn't feel like making the effort to find out. After the New Year, she told herself. She'd reevaluate the situation.

"So what motivated all these changes?" Julia asked, as she came out of the stall. She walked up beside Lauren, and switched on the tap to wash her hands. "Getting ready for the holidays?"

"Well, there's that—but I'm also trying to update my wardrobe—as well as my look," Lauren admitted. She pulled the brush through her hair again, enjoying the way her new cut swung softly into place. Her hair was so much springier and fuller now that it was shorter.

"Well, you've done a fantastic job," Julia told her. "The change is remarkable."

Lauren gave her a grateful smile, and glanced back at her reflection. She had to admit, she thought so, too. Funny how something as simple as wearing new colors and different styles could make a person be noticed so much more. Her smile turned wry. Or at least, be noticed by the other women.

Julia took out her compact to powder her nose. Lauren decided to freshen her makeup, too. She put away her brush, and pulled out the Beckoning Berry lipstick that Jay had stipulated for daytime wear. Until Jay had educated her, Lauren hadn't even realized there was a difference in the makeup used during the day and at night. She'd certainly never had a lipstick that was applied with a tiny sponge at the end of a stick.

She'd learned a lot in the past week or so from her friend. How to exfoliate—and to rejuvenate her skin. How to apply eyeliner and shadow correctly. How to mix and match her wardrobe—and the breast-enhancing qualities of an underwire bra. How to tweeze, pluck, shave and wax—in several excruciatingly painful steps.

If only she could learn Jay's secret for attracting men. "Smile at them more—gaze into their eyes—be friendly," Jay had urged her. So Lauren smiled, and gazed and waved at just about every man that passed. The results so far hadn't been good. In fact, they were practically nil. Although, for a while there, she thought as she slowly began outlining her upper lip, she'd had high hopes of Frank Stephens from accounting.

She'd run into Frank in the lobby a couple of days ago, and he'd accompanied her all the way to the executive suites, chatting about some of the finer restaurants he'd discovered in the city. She'd been sure he was leading up to asking her out—but then Rafe had come into the room and immediately joined their conversation. He'd invited Frank into his office to give him the number of a new bistro on the Loop, and, when they'd returned, Frank had passed Lauren with barely a nod.

With a sigh, she glanced at Julia, who was still powdering her small straight nose. Men definitely noticed Julia. Maybe she could shed some light on what Lauren was doing wrong. "You know, you and a couple of the other women have said something to me about my new clothes, but the men around here haven't noticed a thing."

"Oh, they've noticed all right," Julia assured her, meeting her eyes in the mirror. "I saw Ken Lawson just stand there and stare after you for a full thirty seconds when you passed us in the hall the other day."

Lauren frowned at a chip in her Pick Me! Pink nail polish. Ken was another one that she'd thought might be interested. He'd been very friendly on the day she'd worn her charcoal wrap dress, the one that showed a tiny bit of décolletage. "I'd hoped he'd ask me out," she admitted, "but nothing ever came of it." She turned back to the mirror.

"That's no surprise." Julia closed her case with a tiny snap. "Isn't Rafe his supervisor?"

Lauren paused, lifting the lipstick from her mouth to give the blonde a questioning frown in the mirror. "Yes— but what does that have to do with it?" she asked, then started to color her lower lip, carefully working toward the corner.

"I suspect, just about everything," Julia drawled. "I heard through the grapevine that Rafe has put the word out that dating you isn't what he terms, 'a smart, career move.'"

Lauren's hand jerked, smearing a bright line of Beckoning Berry across her cheek. A flush of anger rose beneath it.

"Why that—that—" Lauren couldn't think of a word bad enough to describe her devious boss.

Julia tried to help her out. "Jerk? Beast? Dirty dog?"

"Every one of those!" Lauren declared, between gritted teeth.

Julia gave her a curious look. "Do you think Rafe's warning the other men off because he's interested in you?"

"Hah! All Rafe Mitchell is interested in is having things his own way." Lauren yanked a paper towel out of the holder and wet it, then leaned closer to the mirror. "You hit it on the head with the dirty dog label," she said, scrubbing furiously at the red mark on her cheek. "He's like a dog with a bone—and not a bone that he even wants to gnaw on himself. All he wants to do is bury it somewhere, so he doesn't have to worry about it," she added bitterly, remembering the comment he'd made about her not understanding men.

Julia's blue eyes sparkled with amusement. "So what are you going to do?"

"There's only one thing I can do," Lauren told her. She tossed her lipstick in her purse and clicked her bag closed. "I'm taking the rest of the day off and I'm going shopping."

Julia's eyes widened. "I agree that shopping is the answer to most of a woman's woes, but won't Rafe get angry if you do that?''

"He'd better not," Lauren said grimly. "I'm doing this shopping for him."

The rescheduled meeting between Rafe, Kane and Lauren had just ended a few days later, when Lauren asked to be excused, saying she had a few phone calls to make.

Both men nodded in agreement. Rafe glanced at her as she gathered up her papers. She was gnawing on her lower lip, a preoccupied frown in her eyes. He shifted his gaze to Kane, who'd been scanning the financial prospectus Rafe had prepared on Bartlett International, and discovered Kane was looking at her, too. Rafe leaned back in his chair, watching Kane watch Lauren...and sighed.

He was getting tired of watching men watch Lauren. All week it had been happening. Men kept appearing, popping out of their offices like cockroaches in a two-star restaurant every time she passed.

He'd caught James Griffin from the advertising firm they dealt with, shooting her a sidelong glance as she passed him in the lobby. He'd seen Nick Murray giving her legs the once-over as she stepped into the elevator. Even the janitor, old Artie Dodge—who was eighty-five if he was a day—had paused while mopping up the hall floor to gawk after her. Rafe couldn't blame him. The sweet, slightly shy smile she'd bestowed on the old guy had made the whole place light up.

Yep, she was stirring up men everywhere. And it was really starting to bug him. One of the roaches had even tried to trail her into the executive suite. Rafe had been forced to take Frank Stephens into his office and, with a thin smile and a firm pat on the back, had let the other man know he'd appreciate it if he'd keep his mind on business—and off Rafe's secretary. He'd had to be equally blunt with Ken Lawson—a notorious flirt—and a couple of the other men as well.

But at least, he congratulated himself, it appeared that the word was getting around. He knew for a fact no one from the firm had asked her out, because he'd kept her working late every night as a preventative. That ploy had also stopped anyone who didn't work for Haley, Inc.—like that Leonardo character she still mentioned now and again—from asking her out as well.

Yeah, he'd thought the worst was over. Yet, here was the big boss, checking her out right in front of Rafe as she picked up her papers and headed to the door. Rafe followed Kane's gaze, noting how nicely Lauren's red skirt displayed the trim shape of her hips and bottom as she sashayed across the carpet. Rafe wasn't surprised at all that as soon as she left, Kane glanced at him with a slight smile and said, "She sure looks different. Nice haircut."

"Yeah, her hair looks great," Rafe agreed, not bothering to hide the sarcasm in his voice. It hadn't been her *head* Kane had been staring at. Kane's grin widened and Rafe's back teeth ground together. Okay, obviously something more than sarcasm was called for here.

He decided to introduce a different subject. "How's your search going for your mystery lady?" he asked Kane.

His boss's smile died. "Not so well. The lawyers haven't made any progress yet, and I don't have any new leads." Kane tossed the prospectus aside, and shoved his hands into his pockets. "Maybe I should just give it up."

"No—you can't do that. You need to find her," Rafe told him firmly.

Kane glanced at him in surprise. "But you said I was probably wasting my time. That you didn't think she would welcome my interference."

"Forget what I said. I've changed my mind since last week." Hell, if Lauren could change her whole image in a weekend, surely he could change his mind on something like this. "If you quit now, you'll always be wondering— 'What if? What if?'"

Kane stared at him. "What if what?"

How should he know? Rafe thought, irritated by the question. Couldn't Kane do any of his thinking for himself? "What if...what if she needs help—or the kid does?" he responded with forced inspiration, remembering the comments Kane had made before. "You need to keep on the trail, keep looking for her." *And stop looking at my secretary.*

"I don't think I could stop, even if I wanted to," Kane admitted.

Rafe stiffened in his chair.

"I can't get her off my mind," Kane said. "Wondering who she might be. If she's okay."

Rafe relaxed a little, as he realized Kane was talking about his mystery woman and not Lauren.

Kane stood up, preparing to leave. Rafe rose also and walked him to the door.

"Anyway, let me know if any problems develop with Bartlett," Kane told him. "You and Lauren are going up there next week, aren't you? To finalize the contract?"

Rafe nodded.

"Good. I'll be glad to get this whole thing wrapped up."

He would be, too, Rafe thought as Kane left. Usually he could handle a deal like this with no problem at all. But he couldn't seem to concentrate on work the way he used to. And it was all Lauren's fault.

He settled back at his desk, thinking about what a troublemaker she'd become. Lately, he spent half his time scaring off predatory males—or looking around, watching out for them. But still, he'd expected that—been prepared for it—from the day she'd chopped off her hair to her chin and most of her skirts to her knees.

What he hadn't expected was the effect the changes she'd made would have on him personally.

He didn't like them; he couldn't get used to them. She'd always been there when he'd needed her, so responsive to his needs that he'd never had to think about her. Useful, unnoticeable and quietly eager to please. He missed all that as well as the easygoing camaraderie they used to share. Mentally, he deplored the loss of "the old Lauren."

But physically, his body applauded the changes she'd made. He'd see her and his heart would beat faster. His muscles tensed. Hell, the little Colonel in his pants practically stood up and saluted every time she entered the room.

Logically, Rafe knew there was no real reason for his reaction. She was still just sweet little Lauren. How much of a difference could new clothes make? Apparently, a lot.

Take the suit she was wearing today for instance. The one that Kane had checked out from top to perky bottom. For one thing, the suit was red. Lauren never wore red. She'd always been a pastel or neutral-colored person. But in red...man, did she look good. Her hair looked more golden, more burnished. Her smooth skin had a rosy glow. The color somehow made her eyes—displayed to advantage in her new contacts—look as blue and wide as the ocean. If a man wasn't careful, he could drown in those big eyes.

But Rafe was being careful—very, very careful—not to look at any part of Lauren for too long. Or too closely. Or too hard.

He simply had to stop thinking of her so much. Wondering if her skin could possibly be as soft as it looked. Or her breasts as sweetly curved as her suit made them appear. To quit calculating how long it would take to undo the four small buttons at the front to find out. He had more important things to calculate. Like the profits and losses of this latest merger.

Setting his jaw, he picked up the Bartlett analysis again—just as his door opened.

Rafe looked up. The little troublemaker herself was standing there, looking like a sexy angel in that devil-red suit.

Rafe frowned and leaned back in his chair. She had an oddly guilty look on her face. For disturbing him, no doubt. Well, she should feel guilty. She'd been disturbing him a lot—even before she came in.

"Yeah? What is it?" he asked.

He knew he sounded abrupt. He couldn't help it. Nor could he keep his gaze from fastening on her mouth. She'd bitten off her lipstick. Her lips were now a dusty rose color. Innocently naked, beautifully bare.

He watched that beautiful mouth move as she said, "There's someone here to see you—if you have time. But if you're busy...." She ended on a breathless note, and ran the tip of her tongue nervously across her lips, making them glisten.

Rafe's gut tightened. She hesitated, as if she wanted to add something else, but he couldn't take it anymore. "Yeah—yeah, send them in," he growled. "You've already interrupted me anyway."

He was perversely pleased to see her soft lips press together into a thin line. He answered her affronted look with an impatient frown.

"Fine," she said icily. "I'll do that."

She disappeared.

Two seconds later, Nancy came sailing through the door, a white fur coat wrapped around her shapely figure. The blonde headed straight for him, then made an end run around his desk. With her hands outstretched, she cried, "Rafe! My darling, I love it!"

"You wha—mmph?" His question was stifled by the full lips pressed ardently to his. She'd caught his cheeks between her hands to hold him in place, obviously digging in for a long one, but Rafe grasped her wrists to pull her hands down. He reared back, managing to liberate his tongue, which she'd tried to take hostage.

He grabbed her shoulders, holding her off as he asked, "What are you talking about?"

"You joker, you! I'm talking about *this!*"

She threw open her coat, and thrust out her breasts—which were pretty thrust out to begin with. It took Rafe a moment to notice the golden heart studded with diamonds hanging on a chain between them.

He wasn't quite sure what to say. "Yeah, it's...nice."

"Nice!" She laughed coyly, snuggling her breasts up against his arm. "I simply love your Christmas present!"

"My—? Hell—lo," he said, making a desperate recovery. "I'm surprised you got it so quickly."

"The jeweler sent it over—special delivery." She glanced up at him from beneath lowered lashes, then looked back down at her chest. "I can't believe you were so extravagant. To buy me *Moustier...!*"

Rafe had no idea what *moo-stee-ai* was, but the awe on her face made his hair stand on end. He raked a hand through it, resisting the urge to tug on it. "I can hardly believe it myself," he said sardonically.

"But what makes it truly special, what means more to me than the ten rose-cut diamonds on the front and the fact that the locket itself is twenty-four-carat gold, is what you put inside.''

Rafe's forehead prickled with sweat. ''And that is…?''

''Your picture, silly.'' She clicked the heart open. She peered inside, heaving a bosom-swelling sigh. ''Although I have to admit, I almost didn't recognize you for a moment with that mustache.''

''That—what!''

Forgetting caution, Rafe grabbed the locket and turned it so that he could see in it for himself. His own eyes stared grimly back at him above a thin dark mustache.

''You look so debonair,'' Nancy purred, giving him a quick peck on the chin.

Rafe gritted his teeth. He looked like a villain from a melodrama, damn it! Not only had Lauren used his driver's license picture—which made him look like a criminal to begin with—but she'd inked in a black mustache beneath his nose.

Nancy hugged his arm again, giving an excited little wiggle. ''And the inscription….''

He shut his eyes. God, no! Not an inscrip—

''*Yours forever, Rafey.* Is it true, Rafey darling? Are you *really* mine forever?''

Like hell he was!

He cautiously opened one eye. Nancy was staring soulfully into his face, waiting for him to answer. He knew he had to tell her something, but his tongue felt thick—as if he were about to choke on it. Maybe she'd injured it during her opening-attack kiss.

He swallowed, trying to ease the dryness in his throat. ''I, ah—''

''Rafe! *Honey!*'' another feminine voice trilled.

The hair rose on the back of Rafe's neck. No, Lauren wouldn't…

He looked over Nancy's shoulder at the redhead posing in the doorway. She had on a black leather skirt, high heels and a gold sweater. A black leather coat was slung across her shoulders. A gold heart locket—studded with diamonds—hung between her breasts.

Apparently, Lauren would.

"Hello, Amy," he said, his voice sounding a trifle hollow.

She flung back her head and her long hair rippled down her back. Ignoring the woman still clinging to his arm, Amy shook a playful finger at him. At least it wasn't her middle finger, he noted. Not yet anyway.

"You wicked, naughty boy," she drawled in a Southern accent thicker than syrup congealing on a plate. She sauntered across the carpet like a leopard stalking its prey.

"You're so *sly*." She drew the last word out a good three seconds—just long enough to step in front of Nancy, and with an adroit shift of her hip, bump the other woman aside.

"Hey!" Nancy protested, staggering backward.

Amy continued to ignore her. Moving closer to Rafe, she ran her finger up and down his tie—a finger, he couldn't help but notice, tipped with a lethally long red nail.

She looked up at him from beneath heavy lids. "Let me thank you, sugar, for the gift of your heart," she breathed, and tugged on his tie, trying to pull his mouth down for a kiss.

Rafe instinctively resisted the leash, but she might have succeeded anyway if Nancy hadn't suddenly shrieked, "What!" and pushed her way back between them.

Planting herself in front of Amy, Nancy lifted up her own necklace, dangling it in front of the smaller woman's face. "Yours forever—?"

"Rafey," Amy hissed, her eyes slitting like a cat's.

Both women turned to glare at Rafe.

He cleared his throat, and tried to loosen his tie. "Yeah, well, it seems there's been a slight misunderstanding."

"You'd better believe it, buster," Amy interrupted, her accent suddenly Yankee-crisp.

And from that point on the women did all the talking— in shrill, accusing voices. When Maureen arrived two minutes later, she didn't even bother with a greeting, just joined the others in haranguing him, barely missing a beat.

Eventually, Maureen took off her locket, flung it at him, then headed to the door. Amy ground hers into the carpet with her stiletto heels. Nancy tearfully took her locket off and laid it on his desk.

"Moustier—Moustier!" she kept repeating in between heaving sobs. "I'll never—ever—forgive you." She turned away, then whirled around again and snatched the necklace up. "But maybe I should keep this—as a memento of our time together."

And she followed the other two out, slamming the door behind her.

In the outer office, Lauren sat behind her desk as the women all went past. First Maureen, with her long dark hair streaming behind her. Then Amy raced through like a redheaded brush fire. And finally Nancy drooped by, clutching her locket in her hand.

Seeing Lauren glance at it, the blonde said simply, "It's Moustier," and, giving Lauren's desk a wide berth, glided out the door.

Lauren fought the urge to join the exodus. She sat stalwartly at her desk, waiting for Rafe to appear. His door remained closed. She strained to listen, but couldn't hear a thing from his office. And the longer the silence stretched, the more her doubts seemed to grow.

This had seemed like such a brilliant plan three days ago. A fit revenge for Rafe's unwelcome interference in her life. But now she wasn't so sure. Listening to the melee in his office, she'd felt as if she'd thrown him to the wolves.

Actually, she'd begun having serious second thoughts about the wisdom of her scheme this morning. She would have called the she-wolves off—that is, the women back—to cancel the surprise meeting she'd arranged, if Rafe hadn't gotten so curt with her, arousing her ire all over again.

You haven't done anything wrong, she reminded herself stoutly, wiping her damp palms on her skirt. *He wanted you to shop for him. You did exactly what he said.* It was simply a fortuitous circumstance that his request—and her desire to pay him back for sticking his nose into her business once again—should coincide so conveniently.

Still, it might not be a bad idea to make herself scarce for while, she thought as silence—ominous silence—practically reeked from his office.

Yes, absence right now seemed to be the better part of valor—or however that old saying went, she decided, as she slipped her purse out of her desk drawer. In other words, this would be a good time for a coffee break. Or a visit to the bathroom. Or perhaps she should take the rest of the day off. Yes, that was what she should do. She should go on home. Very quickly.

She tiptoed to the coatrack to remove her coat. She draped it over her arm, and headed for the hallway. She'd made it halfway there when Rafe's door suddenly opened from behind her.

"Going somewhere?" he asked silkily.

Uh-oh. Too late.

Lauren froze, then slowly turned around. Rafe was

standing in his office doorway, one hand gripping the jamb as if he was holding himself back. His dark hair was rumpled. His eyes were filled with such simmering menace that her gaze quickly dropped to his tie. The dark, discreetly striped silk was all twisted up. She wondered if one of the women had yanked on it or something.

She decided not to ask.

He moved, and she flinched. As he began stalking slowly across the carpet, she backed toward her desk at the same pace, trying to behave nonchalantly. She'd read once never to show fear when faced with a dangerous animal. She kept her expression blank.

Still, she breathed a sigh of relief when her desk was between them. She sat down.

"What were you thinking?" he demanded, standing in front of it.

"Thinking?" she repeated, as if she'd never heard the word before.

Rafe's expression indicated he doubted she ever had. "Yeah, thinking." He leaned toward her, planting his hands on her desk. "What's the idea, buying expensive necklaces like that? Moustier's yet—whatever that is," he added in disgust.

Prudently, she leaned back, out of arm's reach. "You said money was no object."

"I didn't mean it literally. And did you have to buy them all the same thing?"

She widened her eyes. "I was merely trying to follow your orders as efficiently as possible."

"You were, were you?" He eyed her, fulminating. "And did I tell you to put in my picture? And draw that damn mustache?"

"No," she conceded. "I thought of those myself. I

know the women are your *good friends*." She met his gaze limpidly. "I didn't want the gifts to seem impersonal."

"They sure as hell didn't—not with that damn inscription you put in. Yours forever, Rafey."

He bit out a four-letter word.

Lauren stiffened, then jumped to her feet. "Don't you swear at me!" she told him. "This is all your fault!"

His eyes almost started from his head. "*My* fault!"

"Yes! You started it—by telling all the men around here to stay away from me!"

"I—oh. That." He straightened, a disconcerted expression on his lean face.

"Yes, that," Lauren mimicked him, her anger kindling higher at his chagrined look.

She marched around her desk to confront him eye-to-eye. Or in this case, eye-to-chin. "How could you do something like that?" she demanded.

He raked his hand through his hair, rumpling it even more. "I was trying to help you...."

"Help me? Help me how? By scaring off every man who might possibly want to know me?" She started to turn away, but he grasped her shoulders, holding her in place.

Bending his knees a little, he tried to meet her gaze. "C'mon, Lauren. You don't want to go out with those guys."

"That's for me to decide. If I ever get the chance," she added bitterly. "I can't believe you'd do something so mean."

Why had he? Lauren wondered. What did he care if she was trying to make herself happy? Her bottom lip quivered—she bit down hard to hold it steady, to hide the sign of weakness. She had to stay strong; not let him get to her. Make her doubt herself.

She tried to pull away, but his hold on her tightened. "I wasn't trying to be mean," he insisted.

His gaze roamed restlessly over her features, then settled on her lips with peculiar intensity. "I just didn't want anyone to hurt you. I wanted to keep you safe. I wanted everything to go back to normal. I—" His voice thickened. "Oh, hell, I just want you."

And his mouth dropped down on hers.

Chapter Nine

Rafe hadn't intended to kiss her. It was an impulsive move—spurred by the tension of their disagreement, of watching her bite on her rosy lip. She'd gotten him all worked up until, as he'd told her, he just couldn't take any more.

But as soon as his mouth closed over hers, Rafe knew that kissing Lauren was one of the smartest things he'd ever done in his life.

The lips quivering beneath his were unbelievably soft. She tasted unbelievably sweet. He wrapped his arms around her slim waist, pulling her closer, then closer still, reveling in the feel of her slender body pressed against his.

He groaned, deep in his throat, as the amazing thought—*this is Lauren!*—kept echoing in his mind.

It felt so natural, and yet so strange, to hold her like this. He knew the feel of her—he'd put his arm across her shoulders, placed his hand behind her back hundreds of times. But he'd never felt her breasts crushed against his chest. Realized how small her waist was between his hands.

He lifted his head to look down at her. Her eyes were shut. Her dark lashes lay against her pink cheeks. Her mouth was swollen, moist and half-parted, inviting more kisses. She stirred drowsily, moving against him, and desire burned hotter.

Sliding a hand through her silky hair, he cupped her head, holding her still as he brought his mouth back to hers. He kissed the corners then nibbled gently on her lower lip. He traced the subtle curve with his tongue, then angled his head to kiss her more deeply, easing her lips apart.

He explored her mouth, wanting to discover all her tender secrets, to eat her up. He teased her shy tongue, coaxing her to play, and for a second, she resisted. Then, with a small moan, she melted against him. Her slim arms stole up around his neck to cling tightly as she tentatively returned the intimate caress. He could feel those four small buttons pressing into his chest, and the buttons of her nipples as well.

Rafe's body grew harder in response. He stifled a groan. He'd kissed dozens of women in his life, but none had ever felt so right—so perfect in his arms.

Because this was *Lauren*....

Oh, mercy—*Rafe* was kissing her! The thought kept ricocheting through Lauren's mind as he leisurely—thoroughly—explored her mouth. She felt dizzy, weightless. Her breathing was ragged and shallow. He tasted so good. The arms around her were so strong. His hold was firm, almost rough, but still she wanted to be closer.

He lifted his mouth from hers, and her head lolled, falling against his shoulder. She could feel his lips roving across her cheeks, following the line of her jaw to her

GET FREE BOOKS and a FREE GIFT
WHEN YOU PLAY THE...

Just scratch off the silver box with a coin. Then check below to see the gifts you get!

SLOT MACHINE GAME!

YES! I have scratched off the silver box. Please send me the 2 free Silhouette Romance® books and gift for which I qualify. I understand I am under no obligation to purchase any books, as explained on the back of this card.

315 SDL DFTT

215 SDL DFTS
(S-R-OS-12/01)

NAME (PLEASE PRINT CLEARLY)

ADDRESS

APT.# CITY

STATE/PROV. ZIP/POSTAL CODE

7	7	7	**Worth TWO FREE BOOKS plus a BONUS Mystery Gift!**
♣	♣	♣	**Worth TWO FREE BOOKS!**
♣	♣	♣	**Worth ONE FREE BOOK!**
🔔	🔔	♣	**TRY AGAIN!**

Visit us online at www.eHarlequin.com

Offer limited to one per household and not valid to current Silhouette Romance® subscribers. All orders subject to approval.

© 2000 HARLEQUIN ENTERPRISES LTD. ® and TM are trademarks owned by Harlequin Books S.A. used under license.

The Silhouette Reader Service™ — Here's how it works:

Accepting your 2 free books and gift places you under no obligation to buy anything. You may keep the books and gift and return the shipping statement marked "cancel." If you do not cancel, about a month later we'll send you 6 additional novels and bill you just $3.15 each in the U.S., or $3.50 each in Canada, plus 25¢ shipping & handling per book and applicable taxes if any.* That's the complete price and — compared to cover prices of $3.99 each in the U.S. and $4.50 each in Canada — it's quite a bargain! You may cancel at any time, but if you choose to continue, every month we'll send you 6 more books, which you may either purchase at the discount price or return to us and cancel your subscription.

*Terms and prices subject to change without notice. Sales tax applicable in N.Y. Canadian residents will be charged applicable provincial taxes and GST.

If offer card is missing write to: Silhouette Reader Service, 3010 Walden Ave., P.O. Box 1867, Buffalo NY 14240-1867

BUSINESS REPLY MAIL

FIRST-CLASS MAIL   PERMIT NO. 717-003   BUFFALO, NY

POSTAGE WILL BE PAID BY ADDRESSEE

SILHOUETTE READER SERVICE
3010 WALDEN AVE
PO BOX 1867
BUFFALO NY 14240-9952

NO POSTAGE
NECESSARY
IF MAILED
IN THE
UNITED STATES

neck. She moaned as he kissed her gently just beneath her ear. Her eyes stayed shut.

She didn't want to see—she only wanted to feel, to savor the feeling building inside her. The yearning ache tightening like a spring low in her belly as his mouth returned to hers. He was so hot—radiating a heat that burned right through his shirt, right through her suit. Right through her skin. And yet she shivered as his large hand stroked down her back in a slow, lulling caress over her red suit.

Blindly, she lifted her hand to stroke his face, her fingertips tingling at the raspy feel of his jaw. She threaded her fingers through his hair, combing it back, enjoying the way the soft strands tickled as they slid between her fingers. His shoulders were so broad, his chest so hard and muscular. She'd kissed a few men in her life—none had ever made her feel like this. As if her legs had turned to jelly, and the only thing holding her up was her desperate clasp around his neck and his strong arm locked around her waist.

His mouth drew on hers. This time his kiss was so deep it stole her breath, her thoughts, until all she was conscious of was him.

Rafe. Consuming her—burning her up with desire.

He ran a seeking, insistent hand over her hip and up to her waist. Her breasts rubbed against his chest with each movement of his body, and the subtle friction made her nipples peak sharply. The need for him to touch her there kept building—growing—until, when his thumb finally stroked her nipple, she almost convulsed in urgent relief.

"No," she moaned, breaking away.

She backed away unsteadily, bumping into her desk. She leaned on it, lifting a hand to cover her eyes as they fluttered open. The light hurt them. The sight of Rafe's face hurt, too.

He looked like a stranger. Beneath heavy lids his dark gaze was intent, hungry. His skin was flushed, pulled tautly over his strong bones as he reached out for her. "Lauren—"

"No!" she said again, evading his hands.

He paused, his brows drawing down in a frown, his mouth tightening. His lips looked swollen and red. Lauren knew hers must be, too. Her lips felt numb as she said, "I don't want this."

The words were ragged, her chest was heaving as if she'd just run a race. She gulped in air, trying to steady her voice as she forced herself to meet his gaze. "This is just a game to you—one that I refuse to play. I won't be one of your women."

He didn't move. He didn't need to. He just stood there, the hungry passion in his eyes a more persuasive argument than words could ever be.

But he wasn't going to destroy her resolve; she'd come too far to let that happen. So she gathered up her purse and coat and started walking on legs that felt like rubber, heading toward a door that suddenly seemed a hundred miles away.

Finally she made it. She reached the threshold—wobbled—then regained her balance and walked out the door.

Rafe watched her disappear. He drew a deep breath, then blew it out again. Her abrupt withdrawal had stunned him—but that wobble made him smile. It told him she'd been just as shaken up as he was...and he was glad. Because with that kiss, everything had clicked into place, became perfectly clear.

He wanted Lauren. Had probably wanted her for months without realizing it.

As for Lauren, she'd changed her image, her whole outlook, because she wanted a man. And now she'd found one.

Him.

It was the perfect win-win situation.

Not that she'd admit that, he knew. At least not right away. Her final remark had made it more than clear that she didn't want to want him. Lauren was on a quest to find some dream man—dream relationship—that existed only in *her* dreams. It was her idealistic naïveté that made her desire marriage. She was too inexperienced to know that forever wasn't possible.

But he *was* experienced—not that he ran around as much as she obviously thought he did judging by her remark about not becoming one of his "women." He dated plenty of women—he went to bed with only a few. To those few he was faithful while the affair lasted, and he'd be faithful to Lauren while theirs lasted, too.

But it wouldn't last forever. Nothing ever did. Although he'd never felt such a hungry, yearning desire for a woman before, he knew the need would fade. It was bound to. And then—if he handled things very, very carefully—they could simply return to being friends, the way they'd been before this whole thing had started.

Yeah, it all made perfect sense. All he had to do was assuage her qualms—and her apparent anger with him as well—and they could begin to enjoy this new dimension in their friendship.

Not that it would be easy—but he'd handled hostile takeovers before. He knew what to do. He'd start by regaining her trust, reminding her of their previous closeness. Good times they'd shared in the past. Then, when she was at ease with him again, he'd move in under her guard.

And make love to her with a thoroughness she'd never imagined in her wildest dreams.

Yeah, Lauren would discover that when it came to takeovers, Rafe Mitchell was the master.

Chapter Ten

He was doing it again.

Lauren didn't need to look up from the cost analysis she'd been studying to know Rafe's eyes were on her as she sat across his desk from him. She could feel his gaze moving over her body like a lingering caress, leaving a rising tide of warmth in its wake.

She fought to keep her expression blank. She resisted the urge to shift in her chair or yank the hem of her emerald knit dress down over her knees. She subdued the need to fiddle with the tiny black buttons at her breast to make sure they were still securely fastened.

Instead, she kept her eyes fixed on the row of numbers marching across the page. Until finally—thankfully!—his attention returned to the contract in his hand.

Lauren breathed a silent sigh of relief. She continued staring down at the report on her lap, but her mind kept revolving around Rafe and the new game he was playing.

Ever since that kiss two days ago, things had changed between them. She'd told him she didn't want to be one of his women, and he seemed to have accepted that with good grace. On the surface, he appeared to be complying with her decision to keep things platonic between them.

The only problem was, words like *accept* and *comply* weren't even in Rafe's vocabulary. As for good grace— ha! It wasn't like him not to mention that kiss—to tease her about it a little. But he hadn't. Not once.

At first, she'd thought that was a good thing. She'd been grateful he hadn't brought it up. But then she'd realized he'd launched a more covert campaign. These last couple of days, tension hummed in the air whenever he was near her. She'd catch him looking at her with an unsettling expression in his eyes. She felt like the poor goat in that dinosaur movie, tethered to a stake in a jungle clearing, knowing there was danger just beyond the trees but unable to do anything but wait for the predator to pounce.

Okay, she had to admit, a small secret part of her was flattered by his sudden interest, but a larger, far wiser part was appalled and alarmed. It had been hard enough fighting her weakness for Rafe when he wasn't paying any attention to her. It was doubly—triply!—hard to fight it when he kept sending hungry glances her way.

He had to stop it. Immediately. If she'd learned anything these past couple of weeks—besides how to coordinate her clothes—she'd learned she had to stop herself from making foolish choices, to guard her own heart. She'd changed; but Rafe hadn't. The only thing that was different was his reaction to her new look.

He still wasn't the kind of man who fell in love. He still didn't believe in marriage or forever. In all respects, he was still totally the wrong man to get involved with.

So, as far as she was concerned, he needed to keep his distance. He could just go direct those ''I-want-you-bad'' glances at some other woman. Refill his whole address book with more Nancys, Amys and Maureens.

And, since ignoring him didn't seem to be getting the message across that she just wasn't interested, she'd simply have to say it straight out.

The old Lauren quailed at the thought of trying to discuss such a delicate subject. The new Lauren straightened her shoulders with staunch determination. "Rafe?"

"Hmm?" He didn't look up from his report.

"About that kiss…"

For a moment he didn't move. Then slowly he raised his head until his brown eyes locked with hers. He stared at her with an unreadable expression.

"You know—the one the other day," she stumbled on, unnerved by his uncharacteristic silence—then mentally berated herself. Darn! That sounded as if they kissed constantly. She drew a deep breath, and continued more firmly, "I think that we should discuss it."

His dark brows lifted, and he set the contract down on his desk. He smiled—a small, intrigued smile that made her toes curl in her new leather boots. "You want to discuss our kiss?"

She nodded decisively, secretly stretching her toes again. "Yes—yes, I do."

"All right. I'm willing to do that." He rose to his feet, and moved around his desk. He stood next to it for a second, his hands shoved into his pockets. Then slowly he began circling her chair.

Lauren stiffened, resisting the urge to bleat in protest as he paced around her.

"Where should we start?" he mused, pausing next to her to rub his chin. "Maybe with how good you tasted?"

Heat rose in her face. "No! I meant—"

"Should we talk about that soft little sound you made when I stroked your—"

"*No!*"

"—back?" He met her glare with an innocent look.

She jumped to her feet to confront him. "Of course I don't want to discuss—any of that. I just wanted to tell you that while it was…nice—it meant nothing."

"Nice?"

She nodded. "I think we should just forget about it."

"You brought the kiss up to tell me to forget it?"

"Yes," she said firmly. "I want to make sure you understand that it can't happen again."

"I see." Rafe studied her thoughtfully. "You don't think we're missing a great opportunity here? To get to know each other better?"

"I know you as well as I want to."

"Is that so?" he said in a skeptical tone. "Are you saying you didn't feel anything more than 'nice' when you were in my arms?"

Lauren wanted to say yes. She knew she didn't dare. It would be just like Rafe to call her on the lie. "Maybe. A little more," she temporized. "But just because you took me by surprise."

He took a step toward her, his eyes darkening. "Maybe we should try it again."

She hastily moved back. "Certainly not! As I said, it's never, ever going to happen again."

He watched her for a long moment while Lauren fought to keep her expression firm, her knees from going weak, before finally returning to his chair.

Slowly releasing the breath she'd been holding, Lauren sat down also. He picked up the contract again, and she started to relax.

Until he said without looking at her, "Don't be too sure of that, Lauren. Never-ever can be a long, long time."

Patience, Rafe knew, was a virtue. But he'd never been big in the virtue department—especially when he wanted something.

And he definitely wanted Lauren.

But for several days following her announcement that they were never going to kiss again, he kept everything strictly professional between them. They worked next to each other, discussed contracts, mergers and meetings, and he acted as if nothing had ever happened. He let Lauren maintain a careful distance between them without showing that it bothered him in the least.

But it did.

The most innocent brush of her fingers on his, the slide of silk when she crossed her legs, the subtle scent of her new perfume—all were driving him crazy. Hell, he couldn't even listen to her assess stock options in her serious little voice without wanting to drag her across his desk and show her what a "nice" kiss *really* felt like.

So here he was, four nights later, standing at her door at seven in the evening with intentions that were anything but professional.

He knocked, rubbed his hands against the cold and knocked again. A few seconds later, Lauren opened it.

This time she wasn't wearing a faded sweat suit but a silky blue blouse that darkened her eyes and black pants that made her legs look impossibly long and slender. And this time there wasn't a welcoming smile on her face but a frown as her gaze met his.

"Now, give me a chance to explain," he said, before she could speak. "I'm not here to bug you—and I don't want to fight. I was just out walking my tree, and when we passed your place, I thought you wouldn't mind giving it a glass of water.''

He'd mentioned to her after lunch that he'd pick up a tree after work and bring it over, but she'd politely refused his offer, telling him she'd already made arrangements with friends.

He hadn't believed her. He still didn't. And when he'd seen a small pine, apparently abandoned on a deserted tree lot, he'd known immediately that she would like it. Lauren would never turn away a stray.

But for a long moment—definitely long enough to make him wonder if he'd underestimated the strength of her resistance—she simply stood in the doorway, studying his face.

Then her gaze shifted to the tree by his side...and Rafe knew he had her.

She glanced up at him again, a reluctant smile tugging at her lips. ''Oh, Rafe. Where did you find the poor thing?'' She opened the door wider in a silent invitation to enter.

Tension eased in his chest. She liked it—just as he'd known she would. He pretended to be offended as he picked up his tree again to bring it inside. ''Hey—back off. I'll have you know this is a Chicago tree, city-born and -raised. You have to admit, it's definitely a pine with some attitude.''

''Attitude is right,'' she agreed, looking it over. The tree was only five feet tall—but it was also five feet wide. Its lopsided branches spread out in a pugnacious way as he attempted to cram it through the door. It wasn't that the tree was too large to fit, Lauren decided, it simply appeared determined not to enter. Rafe would bend one stubborn branch, only to have another jump out and catch at the frame. The scent of pine, crisp winter cold and muttered curses soon filled the air.

"Maybe you should set it free," she suggested, rubbing her arms to warm them as she stayed out of the way. "It doesn't seem to want to be domesticated."

"It's going to be—whether it wants to or not." Rafe swore beneath his breath again as a branch whipped across his face and scratched his cheek.

"No, stay back," he ordered, as Lauren moved closer to try to help. "I've wrestled these things before—in the marines," he elaborated, in an attempt to make her smile. When he succeeded, he smiled himself, feeling a glow of warmth spreading inside him.

He finally managed to get the tree through the door, and she quickly shut out the cold. She held the tree for him, struggling not to let it fall, as Rafe shrugged out of his coat and suit jacket, and rolled up his sleeves. He took it back from her, and holding the pine upright in her small hall, shook the snow off its branches. A few needles fell on her wooden floor as well.

"It does need a drink," he conceded. "Why don't you go get your tree stand? I think once we get this thing in water, it'll be fairly well subdued."

Lauren went over to some boxes she'd piled in a corner of her living room, and extracted a tree stand—the same one he'd bought her two years ago, Rafe noticed in silent approval. She'd already begun decorating for Christmas, he saw as he glanced around. Red-and-white-striped candles lined her mantel, a wooden reindeer lay curled by a large basket on her hearth. The scent of cinnamon mixed with—he sniffed—could it be sugar cookies? mingled with the scent of pine.

He took the stand and kept her busy helping him hold the tree up, pouring water in at the base. He didn't want to give her time to remember he wasn't her favorite person at the moment.

"Now that the tree has a drink, how about me?" He looked at her hopefully after they got the tree in the stand.

"Something hot or cold?"

"Something hot would be nice."

Lauren felt her pulse leap as Rafe's gaze dropped to her mouth. "I'll make some tea," she said quickly and hurried out of the room.

Why had she let him in? she asked herself as she took a cup out of the cupboard and slammed the door shut. Why was it so hard to say no to the man?

She filled the cup with water and shoved it in the microwave. What she should have said was, "It's a lovely gesture, Rafe, but no thank you." Did he think he could just waltz in here with a tree, and she'd fall helplessly at his feet like—like those pine needles? She took the cup back out. Just because he'd done something so sweet, so charming, so—

She yanked open the tea canister. Well, she wouldn't give in. She wasn't a fool. She dunked a tea bag—up and down, up and down—in the water, then tossed the bag in the trash. Picking up the cup and a tray of appetizers she'd made earlier, she marched into the living room—and slowed to a stop.

Rafe was lying on his stomach on her living-room floor, tightening the tree stand, his head almost buried beneath the tree's branches. Helplessly, her gaze traveled over his long legs, up past his flat masculine butt, to his wide shoulders. The muscles in his back and biceps strained against his shirt as he twisted the clamp tighter on that broad, belligerent, *beautiful* pine.

Lauren bit her lip and looked away.

"I'd better get out my ornaments," she said huskily, setting the cup and platter down on the coffee table.

"Oh, yeah. That reminds me...." Rafe climbed out from under the tree and stood up, briskly wiping his hands together. "I left something in the car."

With a few quick strides he headed out the door. If she knew what was good for her, she'd bar and lock it behind him, Lauren thought crossly. But instead she watched from the doorway as he raced down the steps, took something from his trunk, then bounded up the stairs again, two at a time.

He wasn't even breathing hard when he reached her. Shutting the door behind him, he handed her two packages.

"What are these?" She looked at them in surprise.

"Your Christmas presents."

She glanced at him suspiciously. "You've never given me presents before."

"So, this is a first." He widened his eyes in mock innocence. "They're just a couple things I picked up while I was out shopping."

"Shopping?" she repeated. "You?"

"I may not shop as creatively as you," Rafe said wryly, remembering her most recent shopping spree—the one that had almost gotten him killed, "but I do my best. C'mon, Lauren, it's no big deal. Open them."

As he'd hoped, her curiosity overcame her misgivings. She went into the living room and he followed. Leaning his shoulder against the doorjamb, he crossed his arms as he watched her.

She sat on the couch and placed the smaller present next to her. Setting the larger on her lap, she carefully untaped the silver foil paper, then folded it before laying it neatly aside. She opened the flat wooden box.

"A chess set!" Lauren looked down at the pieces neatly

lining the case. Half were in clear crystal, the other half in frosted glass. "They're wonderful, Rafe…" She glanced up at him. "…but I don't know how to play."

"I'll teach you."

The husky note in his deep voice—the promise in his eyes—made Lauren drop her gaze. With an incomprehensible murmur of thanks, she set the box aside.

Thankful to have something to distract her from his intent stare, she unwrapped the second present. This time the box beneath the foil was white cardboard. She opened it—then gasped, her lips parting in wonder. "Oh, Rafe…"

Cradled in a cloud of pink tissue was a tree-top angel. Carefully, Lauren lifted her free of the box.

The angel's gown was exquisite. Like a white lace snowflake, it drifted around the small body, draping arms that were outstretched in joy.

Golden hair framed the angel's creamy porcelain face. Her painted eyes were blue, her cheeks were tinted a delicate pink. Her rosy lips curved up in a gentle smile that looked appealingly human for such a heavenly little being.

Just looking at her made Lauren smile, too. She swallowed a lump in her throat and touched a finger to one tiny hand. "She's beautiful, Rafe," she said huskily.

"I'm glad you like her," Rafe replied. And he meant it. The happiness on Lauren's face pleased him more than he expected. As soon as he'd caught sight of the angel looking down on him from a tree in a store window downtown, he'd thought of her. He'd immediately bought it, glad to find something she'd enjoy.

Especially since she'd worked so hard on *his* present.

For the past two days—while she was busy ignoring him—he'd reviewed everything that had happened recently, trying to pinpoint exactly where he'd gone wrong in his dealings with her lately. He'd thought hardest about the evening all the trouble had started—the first evening he'd come over to her house. And suddenly he'd remembered the sweater she'd been knitting.

He'd been too preoccupied to think much about it then, but over the past two days he'd thought about it a lot.

It had been big. Too big for a woman. It might be for her new friend Jay, but he didn't think so. Dark brown was a color Rafe wore often—the same color as the scarf she'd made for him last year. Adding all the evidence together, he'd become almost positive that she'd been making it for him. She'd gone to a lot of trouble, knitting a sweater like that, and he didn't want to deprive her of the joy of giving it to him. But realizing that she might feel awkward about handing it over with everything that had happened lately, he decided to make it easier for her.

"Don't you have something for me?" he urged, in a broad hint.

"Oh! Oh, yes, I do." Reluctantly, she set down the angel, then rose and walked over to an end table by a chair. A pile of wrapped gifts were stacked there. Small gifts, Rafe noticed with a slight frown. Way too small to be a sweater, and all approximately the same size.

She picked one at random, and handed it to him. He opened it up. A gold pen was inside.

He looked up at her. "A pen?"

"Don't you like it?"

"Yeah, yeah—it's great, it's just—" He frowned. "Wasn't that sweater you were making for me?"

Her eyes shifted, as if she was going to lie. But then she admitted stiffly, "It was. But I changed my mind."

Aha! Triumph surged through Rafe making him almost light-headed. So she *had* made it for him! "C'mon, Laurie," he coaxed. "It's not fair to change your mind and not give it to me. I'd really like it."

Lauren stared at his amused eyes for a moment, then her gaze dropped to the confident smile on his mouth. "All right," she said woodenly. "Then you can have it."

She walked over to a basket on her hearth and pulled out a big brown ball. She tossed it to him.

Rafe caught it automatically, and stared down at the yarn ball in surprise. "This is my sweater?"

"I made a mistake while knitting it. I corrected the error."

"That was some mistake," Rafe said dryly, "and some correction."

Damn, the lady could hold one mean grudge. For the first time he realized that getting Lauren to change her mind about things wasn't going to be as easy as he'd first thought. He glanced at her. "Lauren—"

The doorbell rang.

"Oh, the others must be here." She walked to the door.

Until that moment, Rafe hadn't believed Lauren's story—that she'd invited others to help at a tree-trimming party. But obviously, he decided as a small, dark-haired woman and a tall blond man entered the apartment, he'd been wrong.

"Hope we're not late," the woman began, "Sam just got back from the store, and— Oh!" She broke off at the sight of Rafe and gave Lauren a sidelong glance. "You must be—"

"Rafe," he supplied, setting down his pen and ball of wool and stepping forward with his hand held out. "And you're—?"

"This is Jay, Rafe. Jay Leonardo," Lauren interjected, not meeting his eyes. "I know you've heard me mention her. And this is her fiancé, Sam McNally."

So this was the Jay she'd been dangling before him, Rafe thought. He should have known. He couldn't wait to tease Lauren about her small deception. To make her squirm a little about—well, not telling a lie exactly, but definitely letting a misconception stand.

"Glad to meet you." Rafe shook hands with the couple. Suddenly things were looking up.

The bell rang again.

This time when Lauren answered it, a pine was standing there. A huge, majestic tree with dense, gleaming green needles.

A man peered around one of the branches. "Lauren?" he said.

Chapter Eleven

It didn't bother Rafe that another tree had turned up on Lauren's doorstep. He liked trees; especially pines. But he didn't feel quite as tolerant about the man attached to this one.

The guy had dark hair and light-colored eyes. Rafe instinctively sized him up as he would another boxer in the ring, instantly recognizing an opponent. Because from the moment Lauren opened the door, the stranger didn't take his eyes off her.

Rafe glared at him, but the sap didn't notice. He was too busy trying to score points.

"Here it is, just like I promised," he told Lauren, sounding as smug as if he'd hunted the tree down and shot it, rather than buying it off a local tree lot.

And without waiting for an invitation—or giving her a chance to explain that there was already a tree on the premises, he pulled it inside.

To Rafe's disgust, the big tree slid smoothly through the

doorway with nary a struggle. He'd never seen such a passive pine.

As the stranger tilted it upright again, Rafe stepped forward to help, an expression of sympathy on his face. "Hey, tough luck, pal. It seems you've gone to a lot of trouble for nothing. Lauren already has a Christmas tree."

The guy's head whipped up to stare at him as if he'd just realized there were other people in the room beside Lauren. He eyed Rafe up and down. "And you are…?"

"Rafe Mitchell."

"Rafe's my boss," Lauren told the newcomer as she closed the door. And she politely explained to Rafe, "This is Jeff Ingram. Jeff just moved into the apartment downstairs a couple of weeks ago. You remember Jay and Sam, don't you, Jeff?"

Ingram nodded and smiled at the couple. But he didn't smile at Rafe. The two men simply exchanged nods and measuring looks.

"So you're Lauren's boss, are you?" Ingram drawled.

"Yep, I'm the lucky man," Rafe replied with a smile that was as false as it was wide. He stepped behind Lauren, establishing a silent claim. "I'm her boss—and also her very good friend."

Lauren jerked around at that and gave him a wary look. Then she moved away to stand by Jay, who was perched on the couch, watching the exchange with great interest. Next to her, Sam was eyeing the tray of appetizers.

Ingram looked at Lauren again, saying with a reproachful note in his voice, "I thought you said you didn't have a tree yet?"

She spread her hands in apology. "I didn't. Rafe surprised me." As she spoke, she gestured at Rafe's tree.

Everyone turned to look in that direction. Rafe's tree

squatted in the corner, bare branches poking out hostilely as if daring anyone to approach.

"What an...interesting tree," Jay said, amusement dancing in her eyes.

"Different," was Sam's succinct contribution.

Ingram was less tactful. "The branches look a little dry. You'd better not put any lights on it." He glanced at Lauren again and shook his tree enticingly, making the branches whisper. "In fact, are you sure you don't want this one?"

For a fleeting second, Rafe's eyes met Lauren's. Then he turned away, pretending to study the appetizer tray. He picked up a cracker dabbed with cream cheese, and threw it in his mouth, telling himself her decision didn't concern him in the least.

He couldn't really blame her for choosing Ingram's tree. Rafe had brought the scraggliest tree he could find to make her laugh. Even Charlie Brown wouldn't have given it a second glance. He kept his expression blank, waiting for her to accept the bigger pine.

From the corner of his eyes, he watched as she bit her lip in indecision. Then she clasped her hands in front of her, apparently reaching a decision.

"Your tree is beautiful," she told Ingram, her soft voice earnest and sincere. "I'd love for others to have the chance to enjoy it, too. Since the smaller tree is already up, would you mind if we take yours down to the women's shelter? Then I can enjoy it when I'm there and everyone else can, too."

Ingram didn't look thrilled at the suggestion, but when Jay exclaimed, "What a great idea!" he gave in with a shrug.

"Okay, I'll run it over there tomorrow. Let me take it back down to my truck."

His dissatisfied expression eased as Lauren immediately suggested, "Why don't we all go and take it over right now? I'd love to see the children's faces when we bring it in."

"Me, too." Jay jumped to her feet and began gathering up her coat and scarf. Sam reluctantly rose also, abandoning the depleted appetizer tray to help her put them on.

Rafe decided not to join the party. Watching Ingram play Mr. Bountiful in front of a bunch of kids was more than his stomach could take on a couple of crackers and cheese.

"Well, I have to take off. Nice meeting everyone." He picked up his pen and coat, then reached for his yarn ball, tucking it under his arm.

Ingram lifted his brows. "What's that?"

"It's my sweater," Rafe told him. "Lauren made it for me."

Ignoring the other man's surprised expression and the sudden flush of color in Lauren's cheeks, Rafe headed to the door.

A chorus of farewells followed him. If Lauren's sounded rather choked—and Ingram's especially hearty—Rafe didn't let it bother him as he strode down the stairs and out to his car.

All in all, he was fairly satisfied with the night's work, he decided as he unlocked his car door. He might not have won the war yet, but he'd held his own in the opening skirmish.

The angel—and even the chess set—had been a big hit with Lauren. He didn't like leaving before Ingram, but the guy wouldn't have the opportunity to put too many moves on her at a women's shelter, especially with Jay and her silent shadow along. And when Lauren came home again it would be *his* tree—not Ingram's—that she'd see in her living room, reminding her of him.

Yep, it had been a fairly productive night. He wasn't even sorry that the others had appeared. Now that he knew what he was up against, he'd simply have to alter his strategy a bit.

He pulled out into the street, mulling that over. Lauren kept complicating the issue. First, with all those fantasies about love and marriage. Then, by denying that their kiss had meant anything to her. Now, she'd entrenched herself in her apartment and surrounded herself with her entourage—Jay, Sam and sappy Jeff—hoping to keep Rafe at bay.

He had to convince her to quit hiding from the truth. To admit that she wasn't as immune to his kiss—to him—as she pretended to be. Once she did that, then he was positive he could get her to agree to an affair and to putting thoughts of marriage behind her.

So, what he needed to do was to lure her out into the open. Invite her to a place where she wouldn't be expecting anything romantic and then slip in under her guard.

And he knew just the place to do it.

"A hockey game?" Lauren regarded her boss doubtfully over the laptop computer she'd set on his desk. They'd been reviewing the Bartlett project in preparation for their trip, when Rafe had casually slipped in the invitation. "You're asking me to watch a bunch of grown men skate around trying to hit a little ball with crooked clubs?"

Rafe gave a long-suffering sigh. Leaning back in his chair, he looked up at the ceiling as if asking for patience. "I've told you before, Lauren. They hit pucks—not balls. And they do it with hockey sticks."

"I see." Okay, now she knew the correct terms to use

when describing hockey players' balls and clubs. What he still hadn't told her was what was behind this sudden invitation.

She didn't trust Rafe, and she especially didn't trust him when he was being casual. "You've never asked me to a hockey game before."

"We've done a lot of things lately that we've never done before," he murmured.

Lauren felt a rush of heat in her cheeks as she thought about their kiss. But before she could say anything he added, "Kane was supposed to take Joe and Norma Benton to this game, but he can't make it so I'm standing in for him. He suggested I take a date since Norma will feel more comfortable with another woman there to talk to."

Lauren knew the Bentons were long-time clients of the firm and that Kane or Rafe often entertained them by taking them to sports events. But she'd certainly never gone along before. "Why me?" she persisted.

He gave her a sardonic glance. "Primarily because the women I'd normally ask aren't speaking to me anymore since your necklace stunt. I figure since you caused the problem, it's only fair for you to help me out. Besides, it will give us a chance to put all this recent unpleasantness behind us. Get back on a friendlier, more normal footing like we did the other night."

The other night had been nice, Lauren admitted. She loved the angel and chess set that he'd given her, and his tree had made her smile. He'd also been a good sport about the yarn ball, and most importantly, not once had he made a sexual move toward her.

Which was exactly what she wanted, she reminded herself, stifling the small pang the thought caused. Especially since her plan finally seemed to be progressing. She'd had fun with Jeff, taking the tree to the women's shelter, seeing the excitement on the children's faces. He might even have kissed her good-night, if Jay and Sam hadn't been there too when he'd dropped her off. And she'd bet that, to Jeff, a kiss meant more than it did to Rafe.

No, there wasn't one tangible thing she could accuse Rafe of doing or saying that was out of line since their talk. Still, maybe it was all her imagination—heaven knew, she had a vivid one—but she couldn't help feeling there was more to this sudden invitation than it seemed.

"What should I wear if I go to the hockey tournament?" she asked, testing him.

"It's a game, not a tournament. As for what to wear…" He shrugged. "I dunno. Definitely something warm. Pants—a thick sweater. Sometimes the stadium can get a little chilly."

He went back to studying the report he'd picked up, and she went back to studying him. Thick sweater? Pants? That certainly didn't sound as if he had seduction in mind.

And he probably didn't. *You're getting paranoid,* she scolded herself. This invitation didn't mean a thing.

As if to support her silent conclusion, he glanced up and met her eyes. "Don't look so torn—it's no big deal. If you have plans for tomorrow night or just don't want to go, I'm sure I can find someone else to take."

"I'll go." After all, there was no reason for him to go to so much trouble. Especially since she'd never seen a hockey game. The niggling thought that she'd never wanted to see one surfaced, but she pushed it down again, adding, "I don't have any other plans."

Rafe didn't even bother to look up again. "Good," he said absently. "I'll pick you up at six."

Chapter Twelve

Lauren could feel the excitement in the crisp air as they joined the crowd pouring into the United Arena. She drew a deep breath, letting it shiver through her as she hugged her coat tighter around her body.

Rafe glanced down at her. "Are you cold?" he asked, and took her hand, feeling her fingers. "Where are your gloves?"

"I forgot them," she admitted. He must have forgotten his, too. His fingers were bare. They felt warm and good wrapped around hers. Too good. Alarmed at how his touch tingled through her, she started to pull way, but his grip tightened.

"Don't want to lose you," he murmured in response to her questioning glance. "There's quite a crowd here tonight."

There certainly was, Lauren decided, and since she didn't want to lose him either—or make a big deal about it—she let him hold her hand as they headed down a wide hallway.

She glanced at the people streaming past. "Almost everyone is wearing black." She looked at Rafe's shirt, revealed beneath his open black leather jacket. "Even you."

He stopped in his tracks, pulling her to a halt beside him. Ignoring the people eddying around them, he made a big production of looking her up and down. "Uh-oh," he said ominously.

Lauren knew he was teasing her; he had to be. But she couldn't help looking down at her jeans and blue mohair sweater apprehensively. "What? What's wrong? Did I tear something?"

The lines by his eyes crinkled. "No. I don't think so...here—turn around a minute." He whirled her around to check out her backside.

Lauren quickly whirled around again. "Rafe!"

He was shaking his head. "No, that's not it. It's worse. Much, much worse." His voice was full of doom. "You're wearing the opposition colors. I'm not sure I want to sit by you."

"So don't," she said tartly. She started to walk away, only to be tugged back by his hold on her hand.

"I have to." He started walking again, giving her a sidelong glance. "Numbered seats you know."

He chuckled as she muttered, "Very funny."

"Besides," he added, as he led her through a doorway and down a series of steps, "these are really good ones."

They *were* good seats, Lauren silently agreed, located by the players' box and right above the glass overlooking the rink.

"Where are the Bentons?" she asked, as she took off her coat.

Rafe shrugged. "Joe mentioned they might be a little

late. They live outside the city, and he and Norma were going out to dinner first.''

Lauren nodded and handed him her coat, which Rafe placed along with his on the empty chair next to him. She sat down next to the players' box.

The Bentons could have eaten here, she thought. The scent of food filled the air, and the noise of the crowd buzzed around them. People were still arriving, but Lauren noticed that the teams were already warming up on the ice. She watched as they swooped and dived, surprised by how graceful they appeared. It reminded her of a ballet—the black team performing on one side of the rink, the blue team on the other. Each pushing their giant black checkers to the nets guarded by the goalie players.

The goalies were like bears, lumbering around, guarding net caves. They wore black, lobster-claw gloves on their hands and snapped at the checker every time it came near.

The warm-ups ended and the teams skated back to their benches. As they clumped into the box on their skates, Lauren realized she was sitting next to the visiting team, the St. Louis Blues. Their uniforms *were* exactly the same color as her sweater, she noticed. It made her feel a certain kinship with the team.

"I'm going to cheer for the Blues," she told Rafe.

He shook his head. "I'm telling you, the Blackhawks will cream them."

"No, they won't."

He gave her a goading look. "Ya wanna bet?"

Lauren could feel heat rising in her cheeks. She knew that he was mocking her, using the same term she'd used when she'd said she wanted a man. The words were definitely a challenge.

She lifted her chin. "Fine. Ten dollars says St. Louis wins."

"Lauren, Lauren, Lauren," he said in a chiding tone. "Aren't you always telling me that gambling is illegal? I was thinking of a more friendly wager."

Suspicion pricked her. "Like what?"

"Oh, I dunno. How 'bout a kiss?"

She turned to stare at him, her eyes narrowing. "So I'd have to kiss you if I lose?"

He widened his eyes in shock. "Of course not. You get to kiss me if you *win*."

She wanted to laugh—she didn't dare. Just the thought of kissing him again made her heart pound. She said as casually as she could, "I don't think so."

He sighed. "All right, we'll do it your way. I get to kiss you if you lose."

She didn't respond to that, trying to pretend she hadn't heard. Leaning closer, he whispered provokingly, "Unless you're...afraid?"

His warm breath caressed her ear, making her stiffen. Darn right she was afraid—but no way was she going to let Mr. Know-It-All know it. She was sure she could manage one quick peck on his cheek if she had to. "You're on."

She was looking over at "her" team again, hoping they'd score lots of points, when her gaze met that of one of the players—a handsome blond with a crooked nose.

He smiled. It was a charming smile, despite the conspicuous gap in his top row of teeth, so Lauren smiled back. He winked. Involuntarily, her smile widened.

"What are you doing?"

She glanced at Rafe, surprised by his annoyed tone. "I'm encouraging my players." She raised her eyebrows, enunciating each word crisply. "Do you have a problem with that?"

Rafe stared into her icy, blue-gray gaze. Hell, yes, he

had a problem! And if that wannabee Romeo didn't quit flirting with her, he'd soon have a problem, too.

He assumed his most earnest, solemn expression. "Yes, I'm afraid I do. You see, Lauren, this is a *hockey* game. Smiling at a player the way you just did—well, it makes him happy. And that weakens him—takes away his fighting edge. I thought you wanted the Blues to win, and now here you are, trying to jinx them."

"Stop it, Rafe," she ordered. She averted her face, but he could see her lips quivering with the effort not to smile. "I know that can't be true."

"Sure it is. If you really want to wish him luck—help him get the right attitude to play—then what you're supposed to do is glare at him. Like this."

He gave a demonstration. Over the top of Lauren's head, he sent the Blues player a look encoded with a silent message. *Back off, Buddy. Or I'll take that stick and wrap it around your throat. And that's a promise.*

"I think it's working," Lauren said dryly from beside him. "He sure looks mad now."

"Yeah, well, it's the least I can do after you tried to take away his competitive edge." Rafe tried to look modest. "Fair is fair, I always say. Now you try it."

He put an encouraging—and possessive—arm across her shoulders. He looked at the player again. *See? In your dreams, pal. She's mine.* "Give him a glare," he urged her, squeezing her shoulders in encouragement.

She glared all right—but in the wrong direction.

"Not at me," Rafe said reproachfully. "I'm not playing hockey tonight. And now you're too late. The anthem is starting." He rose to his feet.

When the anthem finished, the game began. The players hit the puck back and forth on the ice. They hit it in the air. Every fifteen minutes or so, they hit each other with their sticks—or threw the sticks aside to use their fists, punching and pounding. Sometimes even yanking on each other's shirts.

Lauren loved it.

"They're so—so barbaric," she breathed, earning an amused look from Rafe.

Her heart raced along with the Blues as they flew down the ice, pushing the puck ahead of them. She groaned as the menacing Blackhawks stole it back again, taking it the other way. She watched in awe as the row of teenage boys next to Rafe cheered wildly while consuming vast quantities of hot dogs, hamburgers and fries. She enjoyed the raucous music, the dramatic tones of the announcer, the close-ups of the crowds on the overhead monitors. She read each of the warnings on the electronic banner as they flowed past: Watch for Flying Pucks. Use Considerate Language. There was so much to see.

It wasn't until the first intermission when hordes of spectators scrambled to the concession stands that she remembered the Bentons.

"They still aren't here," she pointed out to Rafe. "Do you think something happened?"

He didn't seem concerned. "If it did, Joe has my cellphone number. They probably just got held up."

Lauren was about to suggest that they try to call the couple themselves when the players glided back out onto the rink. Forgetting the Bentons, she tensed as the teenagers started whooping at a Blues player who'd immediately broken away from the pack. He skated frantically toward the net, herding the puck in front of him.

Caught up in the excitement, Lauren desperately shouted, "Score!"—just after the player swung and missed.

The word lingered in the air, falling into one of those

odd pools of silence that sometimes happen in a crowd. Several pairs of eyes turned her way, and the hulking man behind her gave a massive snort. "Give it up, lady. Potocki couldn't score with a hooker on a corner."

"Yes, he could!" Lauren responded loyally, then frowned, uncertain whether she'd defended her player or not.

Rafe grinned at her dilemma, but he also glanced around to give the hulk a warning look. As he settled back into his chair, Rafe's hand closed over hers. Picking it up, he held it snugly in his, atop his warm thigh.

Lauren's breath caught. Rafe seemed absorbed in the game. Maybe he didn't realize he was holding her hand again. Probably he'd done it without thinking. Maybe he'd forgotten she was the one sitting next to him—and not Amy, Maureen or Nancy. Unobtrusively, she tried to slip her fingers from his grasp....

His grip tightened.

She turned and met his eyes. His dark gaze held a mocking gleam. His mouth curved upward in a small, knowing smile as he asked, "What's wrong, Lauren?"

It was another challenge. Just like their bet. And suddenly, it all became clear. Why the Bentons hadn't shown up. Why he'd asked her to the game. As if he'd stated it bluntly, Lauren knew that if she pulled away, she'd be acknowledging that his touch affected her. That she wasn't as indifferent to him as she'd told him she was.

She smiled sweetly. "Nothing's wrong."

She stared at the ice, refusing to look in his direction. What did he think? That she was so susceptible to his charm that she wouldn't be able to resist him? That just because he was holding her hand, she'd fling herself into his arms? How conceited could he get?

She concentrated on the game. Chaos was erupting yet

again. The players skated ever more frantically, graceful yet determined as they chased after their little black disk. Fans screamed at the top of their lungs, urging them on. The heavy man behind her thumped her seat yelling, "Go! Go! Go!" in a hoarse panting voice. The teenagers devised a more complicated chant punctuated with piercing whistles at spaced intervals.

And yet, all Lauren could think about was her hand tucked into Rafe's.

Because now he wasn't simply holding it; he was playing with her fingers. She was wearing a pearl ring—a gift from her mother—which he twisted absently back and forth while he watched the game.

Lauren tried to watch it, too. But then Rafe linked his fingers between hers. He idly rubbed his thumb across her palm in a small circular motion. His thumb was slightly rough, abrasive against her soft skin. It almost tickled—but not quite.

Lauren swallowed as a rush of heat crept from her toes to her cheeks. She'd never realized her palm was so sensitive. He stroked her again, pressing and rubbing. An excited, achy sensation bloomed between her thighs—at her most sensitive, feminine core.

Shocked at her reaction, she jerked her hand out of his, panic propelling her to her feet.

"Hey, lady, could you please sit down?" the fat man behind her bawled in exasperation. "There's a game going on!"

Automatically, she plopped back down. Rafe glanced at her. That small *annoying* smile curved his lips again.

"I'm...hungry," Lauren said defensively. She looked desperately around, and thankfully spotted a vendor near their aisle. Pointing at the pink plastic bag the man was waving about, she announced, "I want some of—of that."

"That" turned out to be cotton candy. Rafe bought her a bag and some peanuts for himself.

Lauren tore open the plastic with trembling fingers. Okay, nothing to worry about here—just a small setback, easily overcome. She could resist Rafe. After all, she had on her Rebellious Red nail polish. All she needed to do was to keep her cool, not let him see that he was getting to her. At least for the moment he was no longer holding her hand. And now she had something else to think about: food.

She pulled off a large wad of fluffy candy and stuffed it in her mouth. For a distressing second it just sat dryly on her tongue—like real cotton—then gradually began to melt.

She tried to concentrate on the sweetness in her mouth, rather than the man calmly munching peanuts beside her. His clean, masculine scent seemed to entice her, inviting her to inhale deeply. His broad shoulder bumped hers companionably—and she fought the urge to lean her cheek against him.

"Another offside. They need to keep their heads in the game."

"They sure do," Lauren agreed—without the least idea of what he was talking about.

She stole a glance at his face, watching his mouth tilt up at the corner as he made another comment about the Blackhawks. Her gaze lifted to his eyes, and she became distracted by the thickness of his dark lashes. And his voice—she really liked his voice. The deep, husky sound of it sent shivers up her spine.

She blinked when suddenly his gaze met hers.

"Want some?" he asked, holding up his peanut bag. He poured a handful into her palm.

Lauren clutched them in her fist, then ate them one at a

time, afraid that if she wasn't careful, she might choke. Her throat felt so tight. When she finished the nuts, she reached into her bag for another chunk of cotton candy. More to keep her hands busy—and out of danger—than because she was hungry.

She pulled loose a sticky clump—and Rafe caught her wrist, lifting the pink tuft to his mouth. He bit down on the candy, tugging it from her fingers. He swallowed and smiled—a heavy-lidded smile that didn't lighten the intense look in his eyes at all.

Then his lips closed over her fingers. He sucked gently, making them tingle. Making her feel dazed.

"Mmm, sweet," he murmured, his breath flowing warmly against her skin. He nibbled his way down to her palm and licked her there. "And salty."

It was erotic—it was crazy. People were cheering and jeering all around them, yet Lauren felt as if she and Rafe were drifting in their own silent, sexy bubble.

He turned her hand and kissed the delicate skin of her wrist, pressing his lips against her fluttering pulse. He nibbled his way to her fingers again, and took the tip of her little finger into his mouth. She could feel the sharp edge of his teeth against the sensitive pad, and then he circled it with his wet tongue. And obviously, her body was totally confused. Her nipples kept tightening, as if they were being rolled and sucked, scraped ever so lightly with his teeth.

She held her breath as he sucked harder. His intent gaze, dark with smoldering passion, met hers as he bit down gently.

Lauren gasped. The crowd roared. Rafe's gaze flared with satisfaction—then flickered past her. He flung himself over her.

His body was heavy and limp. Lauren stiffened in outrage beneath him. Now he'd gone too far! He was lying right on top of her—and this was a public place!

Her face was buried against his shirt. She struggled to turn her head, her voice muffled as she demanded, "Rafe Mitchell, get off of me this instant!" She shoved at his shoulders.

"Give 'im a break, lady!" The fat man bawled from behind her. "He saved you from that puck, didn't he? I think it knocked 'im out."

Chapter Thirteen

"Rafe, I'm so, so sorry."

"You already told me that," *At least ten times,* Rafe added silently, as they walked out to his car. And for the tenth time, he repeated, "And I keep telling you it's okay. It wasn't your fault."

"But I never should have shoved at you like that. I didn't know that you were unconscious—"

"I was stunned, not unconscious."

"I thought that you were—"

"I know. Putting a major move on you. You told me that, too. In front of the security staff in the first-aid room."

And, judging by their broad grins, the men had absolutely loved it. Rafe couldn't blame them. It certainly didn't say much for his seduction technique if Lauren couldn't tell if he was making a move or if he was uncon— a little out of it.

His jaw tightened, which made his head throb. He

picked up his pace, his boots crunching on the icy asphalt as he strode along.

Beside him, Lauren took a little skip to keep up, and slipped her hand through his arm. "Honestly Rafe, I really appreciate what you did." She gave his bicep a grateful squeeze. Her voice was filled with admiration as she added, "And the people at the stadium were so-o-o-o impressed. They showed the whole thing on the overhead monitors, you know. Did you hear the way everyone applauded when you staggered to your feet?"

"Yeah, I was a real hero. Stopping a puck with my head like that." He felt like an idiot. He'd been so involved in kissing Lauren's hand, so enthralled by her breathless response, the darkening passion in her eyes, that he hadn't even seen the puck flying their way until it was almost too late. Instinctively, he'd tried to protect her, barely getting his hand up in time to deflect the puck a little—right to his temple.

He sighed, rubbing the bump. Oh, well. At least it hadn't hit Lauren. And he'd never have to see those thousands of people in the stadium again.

They stopped beside his car. Rafe started to open the car door for her when Lauren held out her hand. "Here— give me your keys. I'm going to drive."

Rafe stared at her. Maybe that puck had hit her after all. Cuz she was talking crazy. "You're not driving my Porsche."

She heaved a loud sigh of exasperation. Her hand remained extended, palm up. She wiggled her fingers demandingly. "Then I'm not getting in the car. You were just knocked—"

"Dazed."

"—out and you're in no condition to drive. It isn't safe."

Rafe tried to outstare her but her eyes didn't waver. He inhaled impatiently. How could he argue about her safety? "Fine. Here." He slapped the keys in her hand.

They both got in. Rafe slumped down in the passenger seat, wincing as she ground the gears starting up. They'd only been driving a few minutes, when Lauren announced she was taking him to the hospital.

Rafe had his gaze glued to the road to help her drive, but he glanced away for a brief second to frown at her. "No, you're not."

"Yes, I am. You've been grimacing in pain for the last half mile."

"That's because you keep riding the clutch! Would you please get your foot off it?"

"Oh. Sorry." She moved her foot. "But I still think you should go to the hospital."

He glared at her. "Well, I don't."

After that, Lauren remained silent. Several minutes later, she parked the car in front of her place and got out, still without speaking. Snow sparkled in the moonlight and stars twinkled overhead. The scent of smoke from a nearby fireplace drifted in the air as they climbed the stairs to her apartment. She unlocked the door and went inside, Rafe following at her heels. She shut the door firmly behind him and immediately began helping him remove his jacket, sliding it down his arms.

His brows rose in surprise. This was a change. He'd expected her to try to hustle him out the door, not to start undressing him. "Lauren?"

Ignoring him, she whipped his coat off and turned to hang it in the closet. "Go into the living room and sit down," she ordered over her shoulder. "I need to turn the heat up in here, then I'll get some ice for that bump. It's the least I can do since you saved my life."

Rafe drew a deep breath, striving for patience. He couldn't believe she was making such a fuss. His foster mothers' attitudes had always been pretty much "if someone's not dead, don't bother me." In the marines, you didn't hold up your troop with minor injuries. But Lauren always had been a softie. He shook his head at her.

"I didn't save your life and I don't need any ice. My head's fine."

"It is, is it?" She turned to face him and crossed her arms, resting her shoulder against the doorjamb. "If it's so fine, then why did you let me drive your precious car?"

His mouth opened, then closed. He wanted to answer her, but damned if he could think of a good reason. "Because you ordered me to give you the keys!" he said finally.

"That was a test. To see how you'd react. You never would have let me drive if you felt one hundred percent okay. Now go sit down while I take off my coat and get out of these shoes. They're wet."

A test, huh? Kind of like *his* test—when he'd kissed her hand at the game to see what her reaction would be. Remembering how her eyes had dilated with passion, his voice thickened. "Lauren—"

She pointed toward the living room. "Sit!"

He watched her disappear into the hallway, then stalked over to the chair next to her couch and sat down. He didn't want ice; he wanted to get on with her seduction. He folded his arms, stretched out his legs and stared moodily at his feet. His shoes were wet, too. And there was a sticky orange stain on one of the toes. He squinted, trying to figure out what it could be. Soda pop, probably, he decided. He vaguely remembered kicking one of the teenagers' cups as he'd thrown himself over Lauren.

He lifted a hand to rub his forehead. Now that he was

sitting still, he realized his head *was* still throbbing—just a little. His hand hurt, too, on his right palm—probably where the puck had struck it.

He lowered his hand as Lauren came back into the room. She'd removed her coat and shoes, but was still wearing her fuzzy blue sweater and jeans. Thick red socks were on her feet. She padded past him into the kitchen. "I'm going to get that ice. Would you like something to drink?"

"No, thanks." He didn't want the ice either, but decided not to tell her that again and start another argument. Fighting with her wasn't part of his plan.

He looked toward the kitchen, narrowing his eyes against the bright light from her table lamp. He could hear water running, the refrigerator door open and close. A few minutes later, she came walking out with an ice bag in her hand. She paused by the lamp and dimmed it.

She must have seen the surprise on his face because she said, "The glare looked like it was bothering you."

Rafe felt the muscles around his eyes relax and realized she'd been right. She came around the chair to stand behind him, and gently placed the bag against his temple.

He flinched, more in reaction to the cold than pain.

"Does it hurt?"

"No." He liked the concern in her voice. Maybe he'd been going about this seduction stuff the wrong way, he thought, relaxing a little. After all, he was in Lauren's apartment—alone with her—and she wanted to take care of him. Why not accept a little TLC?

He leaned his head back but the chair was too low to support his neck, so he straightened again.

"Here—just a minute." For a second, the ice bag slipped as she moved away and he automatically lifted his hand to hold it in place. Then she returned and tucked something behind his neck. Something furry and soft.

"What's that?"

"My teddy bear. Now, lean back." She took the bag again, and gently pulled his head back against the bear. He expected her to step away, but she didn't. She just stood behind him, holding the ice to his bruise, neither of them talking.

"Lauren—"

"Shhh. Just relax."

Her warmth, the dimly lit apartment, the cold bag— okay, he had to admit, it felt good. Very good, as a matter of fact. It felt even better when she lightly, tentatively, began brushing his hair back from his forehead. Her slender fingers soothed him, sifting through his hair, stroking his scalp. Rafe stifled a sigh of mingled relief and pleasure. His eyes drifted shut. He couldn't remember anyone ever fussing over him like this.

"Rafe?"

He opened his eyes a slit. Lauren's face, upside-down from this angle, wore a worried expression as she looked down at him. "Are you sure you don't need a doctor? The medic at the rink said if you feel dizzy or weak you should go get checked out."

"Lauren, I'm fine."

He did feel dizzy and weak, but it had nothing to do with his injury. He didn't need a doctor. He just needed her to keep stroking his hair the way she'd been doing.

And she did. He closed his eyes again. He found himself anticipating each glide of her fingers, each gentle breath she drew. He could smell her perfume, cotton candy and the enticing, womanly scent that was Lauren herself.

He opened his eyes again. She was still looking solemnly down at him, her eyes dark and serious. As she met his gaze she spoke, her voice quivering just a bit. "I'd feel terrible if anything happened to you, Rafe. Especially since you got hurt saving me. It was...scary, when I realized you were really hurt."

Something inside him softened. She sounded so worried. He reached up and curled his hand behind her head. Slowly, he pulled her down until her lips met his in a short, sweet, upside-down kiss.

When he let her go, she eyed him questioningly. "What was that?" she asked softly. "Another challenge?"

"Just a kiss, Lauren." His voice sounded husky, and he cleared his throat. "To thank you for taking care of me."

"I see." She ran her fingers through his hair again, her smoky blue eyes darkening even more. "Well, I forgot to tell you something. The Blues won."

His pulse kicked into overdrive as she slowly bent down to press her soft mouth to his. For a long moment, he didn't move. Then he felt the tip of her upside-down tongue shyly touch his, and heat flooded his body.

He tossed the bag of ice on the floor. Hell, it would have melted in a couple of minutes anyway. "C'mere," he muttered against her mouth.

He caught her wrist, pulling her around the chair, and down onto his lap. Her arm circled his neck and shoulder, and she laid one hand against his chest. He wondered if she could feel his heart pounding beneath her palm as he took her mouth again.

His lips moved along her cheek, and he felt her take a quick breath. "Rafe. Your head—"

"Forget my head." It wasn't the throbbing in his temple that concerned him, but the throbbing in his loins. His mouth closed over hers again and this time he groaned aloud. It felt longer than a few days since he'd held her in his arms. It felt like a lifetime. Kissing her was like coming home. Warm and sweet and welcoming. She tasted like sugar and peanuts. She tasted like she was his.

He wanted to kiss her forever—to kiss her everywhere. Intimately and completely. To feel her melt like cotton candy against his tongue. Without lifting his mouth from hers he slid his hand under her soft sweater, finding the smoother, even softer skin beneath it. He stroked her back, running his fingers down the delicate ridge of her spine. He smoothed his palm over her stomach, then slid his hand higher.

Still kissing her, he cupped her breast. Beneath the lace of her bra, the small bump of her nipple nestled against his palm. His body grew harder as he felt her quiver, heard her make a little moaning sound in her throat. His kiss grew hungrier, his hands more urgent. He didn't want to stop, he couldn't seem to stop—but she put her hands on his cheeks, gently pushing him away.

"Rafe," she whispered against his mouth, her breath sweet and ragged. "Are you sure all this isn't too much for you? What if you have a concussion or something?"

The whispered words jolted him. Warmth spread through him—and a touch of shame. It wasn't herself she was worried about...it was him.

He looked down at her. Her eyes still looked concerned, but they were also cloudy with desire. Passion had softened her features. Her mouth was red, her cheeks pink with sensual heat. Her body felt boneless, warm and yielding as she lay across his lap.

Her fingers stroked the back of his head, gently playing with his hair. She was asking him if he wanted to stop— while making it clear that she wanted to continue.

Looking down into her eyes, he knew all he had to do was to say he was okay, and she'd let him make love to her. In fact, wasn't that what he'd planned to do all along?

To seduce her, to use her desire for him to gain her surrender? To prove to her he was the man that she wanted?

Yeah, he'd subconsciously planned to let the lovemaking come first, the talking after. With any other woman— the more sophisticated ones he'd been with in the past— it wouldn't have been a problem. They'd known the score up-front. They were familiar with the rules of the game.

But Lauren was different. She was special. He cared about her—really cared about her—much more than he'd even realized. He wanted her to be sure she knew what she was doing. He didn't want her to agree to make love with him out of gratitude, because she thought he'd saved her from a damn puck.

With a sigh, he cupped her chin in his hand and met her gaze with his own. "We need to talk."

The resolve in his voice seemed to get through the sensual daze she was in. He felt her stiffen, saw the flush in her cheeks deepen as she removed her arm from around his neck.

When she tried to move away, he held her tight. "I care about you, Lauren. You're special to me. I've never known anyone like you, you're so incredibly sweet." He rubbed his cheek against her soft hair. "I don't want to do anything that might hurt you."

She'd averted her face, but at that, she turned and met his eyes, hers wide and questioning.

He added, "So I want you to be very—very—sure that this is what you want. I don't want you to have any second thoughts, or any regrets, afterward. I want our first time together to be perfect."

Her eyes grew luminous. Her lips softened. "Oh, Rafe—"

"No—" His voice was harsh with the strain of resisting her. He put his fingers against her mouth. "Don't answer me now. I want you to think this all over hard and carefully.''

He stood up, lifting her with him, and set her on her feet. He held her until she was steady, his hands on her shoulders.

He told her, ''We're leaving day after tomorrow for Hillsboro, and by then you'll have had time to make a decision. Whatever it is, you can tell me there, when we're alone. And I promise I'll understand.''

His voice deepened, and he leaned forward to brush his lips lightly against hers, one more time. ''And I also promise that if you choose me, I'll make sure that you won't regret it.''

Chapter Fourteen

I care about you, Lauren. You're special to me.

Every time the memory of Rafe's words drifted through Lauren's mind the next day as she packed for their business trip, her pulse would quicken with happiness.

He'd looked so endearing last night, with his hair sticking up on one side, flattened on the other where the ice had wet it. He'd been so grouchy because that puck had knocked him out. She'd wanted to laugh at him. She'd wanted to take care of him. She'd wanted to put her arms around him and…just love him.

He'd been so tender when he'd kissed her. His eyes so serious when he'd pulled her down onto his lap. His lips had been hungry—his body hard with desire. Yet, he'd stopped her when she'd wanted to continue their lovemaking. He'd told her that she needed time to think.

That wasn't something a man did who was just fooling around, just playing a game. No, she was sure about that. It was something a man did when he was in love.

The thought made her pulse flutter. She'd called Jay, to

tell her what had happened, and her friend had sounded skeptical about Rafe's feelings. But Lauren had just laughed, for once confident in herself as a woman.

Jay liked everything spelled out. She was worried that Rafe still wasn't interested in marriage. But Jay didn't realize that when a person was in love, their feelings changed about everything. Hadn't Lauren's feelings changed when she'd thought he'd been seriously hurt by that puck? She'd realized then that despite her new plan, her new resolve, she still loved him. She'd been ready to make love with him, in fact, despite her one-time resolve to wait until marriage. Love and Rafe were what mattered—not a ceremony.

He'd been so sweet, so tender, so caring about her. So determined that she "think things over." And he'd wanted their first time together to be perfect. Yes, he loved her all right.

So Cinderella preparing for the ball couldn't have been more excited—or more particular—than Lauren was as she packed for their trip.

She chose her favorite blue suit to wear in the morning, deciding it would be comfortable for the car ride, yet would look neat and professional for their first meeting at Bartlett, Inc.

She selected another suit—a prim burgundy—to wear to dinner, but included her "little black dress" as a possible alternative. "All women, no matter their age, shape or economic level, need a little black dress," Jay had told her firmly when they'd gone shopping. "It's good for late-night romance if you team it with a sheer scarf, it's good for funerals if you team it with a black jacket. You can dress it up, you can dress it down."

Or, Lauren thought wryly as she removed it from its hanger, she could wear it as it was and appear almost completely undressed. She'd change into the burgundy suit if dinner ended up being a business affair, she decided, but if just she and Rafe dined together—well, why not the black?

She added it to the case. Then, after hesitating a moment, she went back into her closet, and took down the white box set on top of the one containing her mother's wedding dress.

She opened it and drew out the nightgown inside, letting the silk ripple across her hands in a smooth sensuous flow. She brushed a fold across her cheek, enjoying the material's cool softness. She'd had the gown forever. She'd bought it on a whim when she'd first moved to Chicago. Frightfully expensive, wickedly beautiful, the slim silk sheath was a pure, snowy white.

She'd never worn it. She'd put it up in her closet, to save to wear for that special someone she'd dreamed of finding someday. She'd looked good in it when she'd tried it on in the lingerie store, way before her makeover. She was sure it would look even better on her now.

So she wrapped it in a sheet of tissue paper and put it in her case.

It was a rather large case for a two-night trip, but Rafe didn't mention that when he came to pick her up at dawn the next morning. In fact, he didn't even seem to notice. His gaze met hers with an intent, almost searching look as he took it from her hand.

She thought for a moment he might kiss her, and her breath caught. But then he stepped back.

Lauren felt oddly flustered. She glanced at his face, then quickly looked away again. "How's your head?" she asked hurriedly.

Something in her expression must have pleased him,

because his eyes softened and he smiled. "My bump is gone, but I'm getting dizzy just looking at you."

His gaze skimmed down to her black high heels, then roamed slowly up her legs again to her blue wool suit, buttoned up snugly to reveal just the white lace collar of her blouse. "You look beautiful," he said huskily.

The compliment thrilled her. But it made her self-conscious, too. She wasn't used to hearing things like that from Rafe. She was more accustomed to his teasing. "I've worn this before, just a week ago," she said lightly as they walked to his car.

He put her case in his trunk, then turned back to her. He smiled into her eyes. "And I should have told you then how fantastic you look in it."

Again she felt a thrill. Not quite sure how to respond to this new, charming, "politically correct" version of Rafe she climbed into the car. She tried not to think about the night ahead. What he'd say when he took her in his arms. What would happen after she gave him her answer. She trembled with anticipation.

As if he sensed her tension, Rafe kept the conversation flowing and fixed on business. "This isn't going to be an easy merger," he warned her as they drove out of the city. "Bartlett's people seem to be taking it pretty hard."

That became obvious as soon as they arrived an hour later. The managers greeting them were tense, their expressions strained, as they gathered in the conference room to find out exactly how the takeover would affect them. Their responsibilities, their families, were obviously their main concern. Especially since, in this uncertain economy, new jobs weren't always easy to come by, and mortgages and college tuitions were constantly on the rise.

Lauren knew Rafe wasn't unaware of their plight, but to him, business was business. Any buyout situation

meant restructuring, and since Bartlett had been operating
in the red for quite some time, in this instance the cutbacks
would be severe. Management, as usual, would take the
heaviest hit. Since they'd been in control of the disaster,
they'd be the first to be eliminated.

Many, of course, had already lined up positions else-
where, and a few would be kept on. But still, there were
enough worried expressions in the group to make Lauren's
heart feel heavy. This was the part of her job she liked the
least. She had no problem looking at numbers and rec-
ommending changes. It was much harder looking into peo-
ples' faces and doing the same, knowing that jobs were at
stake.

She did what she could to soften the blow, offering coffee and silent sympathy wherever possible. But when the
day's meetings were concluded she felt drained, and much
of her earlier Cinderella glow had faded.

Rafe, however, appeared elated and full of energy. Taking her arm, he strode briskly to the car to head for the
hotel. "Can you believe it? We covered more today than
I ever thought possible. A brief follow-up session tomorrow, and this project should be in the bag."

He continued to talk about the day's work as they drove,
but the closer they got to the hotel, the harder time Lauren
had concentrating on what he was saying. Her stomach
flipped when the hotel sign came into view—but then he
drove on past.

Her head whipped around to stare back at it. "Rafe!
That was our hotel."

He shook his head. "No—I canceled our reservations
there. I'm taking you to the Chariot. It's much smaller, but
I think you'll prefer it."

The Chariot *was* smaller—it was also very exclusive.
Tucked back from the main road, it wouldn't catch the

attention of many passing tourists, Lauren thought. Nor, she decided as a doorman wearing white gloves ushered them into the lobby, would the average tourist be able to afford the place. Huge vases of flowers were placed throughout the room. Everything gleamed, from the black marble of the concierge's desk, to the Venetian glass in the wall sconces and the chandelier overhead.

Even the hotel manager gleamed, with his sleek black hair and toothpaste smile, as Rafe strode toward the reception desk.

"Mr. Mitchell, how nice to see you again." The man flicked a glance at a waiting bellhop who immediately stepped forward to take their cases. "Mr. Mitchell and his guest will lodge in the west wing," the manager told him.

A small, unpleasant shock ran through Lauren. She wasn't Rafe's guest—they were here on business. But that wasn't quite true either. They'd done business today, but tonight, Rafe had said, would be just for them. She caught the quick evaluating look the bellhop gave her before he led the way to the elevators. There was nothing offensive in the look. Far from it. It was just an impersonal, possibly unconscious, evaluation of her charms. Still, an uneasy feeling crept up her spine.

"This hotel isn't on the company's approved list," she whispered to Rafe as they followed the bellhop.

He gave her a sideways glance, his eyebrows rising. "I'm paying for this, not the corporation."

Lauren was glad that Kane Haley, Inc., wasn't paying for their—their getaway. But she wasn't sure she liked Rafe paying for it either.

Still, it was probably unsophisticated of her to worry about it. These days no one cared if two adults decided to share a room. She was relieved, however, to find that Rafe had booked them separate rooms. She was a private per-

son, and she didn't want to be the source of speculation—
even to a minor degree—for the hotel staff.

Her room was lovely. A tufted, hunter-green sofa sat
near the window, while the bed and the rest of the furniture
were carved of glossy mahogany. Thick, plush beige car-
peting was on the floor, and sparkling mirrors hung above
the dressing table and on the closet doors. There was even
a crystal bowl of fruit on the table near the bed.

After glancing around, undoubtedly to make sure everything was okay, Rafe left to follow the bellhop to another
room across the hall. Lauren didn't even get the chance to
open her case before she heard a knock at her door.

She jumped. Pressing a hand against her chest, she went
to answer it.

She opened her door. "Hey, you," Rafe said softly,
looking down at her.

"Hey, yourself," she responded, melting a little at the
smile in his eyes. When he glanced toward her bed, her
pulse skipped a beat.

He looked back down at her. "Do you want to go somewhere else for dinner, try the dining room here, or…" He
paused. "…have dinner sent to my room?"

His room? She struggled to breathe. She honestly didn't
want to drive anywhere, and she wasn't interested in making an appearance down in the dining room. "Your
room," she decided in a daring rush.

His eyes flared, and his lips curved in a satisfied smile.
"Good choice. Should I go ahead and order? Do you have
any preferences?"

"You decide." Food was the last thing she could think
about right now.

"Come on over then at…" He checked his watch.
"…how 'bout eight?"

She nodded, and he sauntered back across the hall. Lauren shut the door then leaned against it a moment to catch her breath. The other night in his arms she hadn't been so nervous. It's just the anticipation, she told herself. The realization that this was it—The Big Night.

Excitement made her tremble as she dressed for dinner, she told herself. She'd bathed and was in her robe applying her eye makeup when another knock sounded.

Her hand jerked a little. She swallowed, trying to ease her suddenly tight throat. It appeared Rafe was more impatient than she'd realized. She tightened her sash and answered the door.

"Flowers for you, Miss Connor," the bellhop said, cradling a huge vase in his arms.

Lauren's eyes widened. Roses. Red roses. At least two dozen, beautiful, long-stemmed, wonderfully fragrant roses.

No one had ever sent her roses before.

She clasped a hand to her throat and stepped aside as the man came in to set the flowers on a table. She knew a wide smile was on her face as she reached for her purse to tip him. She couldn't help it.

He turned and waved away her offering. "Mr. Mitchell *always* takes care of that. Have a nice evening." With a nod, he went out the door.

Lauren's smile faded a little. Mr. Mitchell always takes care of that? She searched for a card and found one tucked among the green leaves. "For a Beautiful Woman. Rafe." Foolish disappointment pricked her. It was a nice compliment—obviously the only compliment Rafe could think of today. She was glad he thought she was beautiful, but she wished he'd signed the card "Love, Rafe."

Still, just because he hadn't said it yet, didn't mean he didn't feel it. She stroked a silky red petal. Before the night was over, she was certain he'd say the words she was longing to hear.

She went back to getting ready. She smoothed moisturizer on all over her body, then lightly touched what Jay called "hot spots" with perfume. Behind her ears. Between her breasts. Daringly, above the juncture of her thighs. She slipped on black underwear that was nothing more than a few strings of lace with a triangle patch at the front. She put on silky nylons—the really sexy kind that clipped on to garters. She'd never felt so sexy, so seductive in her life!

She couldn't wear a bra. The cut of the black dress didn't allow it. At least having small breasts meant she didn't need much support, she thought, as she drew the spaghetti straps over her shoulders. She looked at herself in the mirror. The front of the dress was fairly modest. The V-neckline was low, but not too much so. The skirt of the dress wasn't too tight, nor was it especially short. The hem swirled just above her knees. No, it was the back that made the dress so daring. She twisted to look at it in the mirror. Talk about inviting a draft! The back was cut low—dipping well past her waist. The white skin of her shoulders and back looked shockingly bare against the black material.

But that was okay. Lauren squared her shoulders and straightened her spine, then stepped into her black heels.

She drew a deep breath and picked up her purse. At eight o'clock precisely, she knocked on Rafe's door.

He immediately opened it.

"Oh!" She stared at his jeans and casual gray pullover shirt.

A wicked smile played around his mouth as his gaze skimmed her body. "Oh, ye-ah," he drawled.

Lauren started to turn away. "I didn't realize—this is too fancy—"

"This is just right." Rafe grabbed her wrist and pulled her into his room. "You look beautiful, Lauren. Really."

There was that word again. But it was okay, she supposed, when there was such warmth in his voice when he said it.

His room was nice, decorated in shades of blue and gold. The bed seemed awfully big, though, to Lauren's wide gaze. It dominated almost half the room. A fire burned in the white marble fireplace. Soft music flowed from the sound system.

Rafe squeezed her fingers. "Would you like some wine before we eat?"

Lauren hated wine. "Sure." It might help relax her.

Still holding her hand, he led her over to the small table in front of the fire, set with white linen, covered dishes and flickering candles.

While he poured the wine, she said, "Thank you for the flowers, Rafe. They're lovely."

"Glad you like them." He handed her a glass. "Are you hungry? Would you like to eat now?"

"Sure." Her voice sounded strange, so she drank some wine to clear it. Her lips almost puckered it tasted so dry. "That would be nice."

He stepped behind her to draw out her chair—and sucked in a breath.

"What?" She glanced over her shoulder at him.

"Nothing." His voice sounded strangled. "That's just—some dress."

Lauren blushed, and he grinned.

They started eating. Lauren was sure the food was good; she just couldn't seem to taste it. The way her stomach was knotting up the dinner could be cardboard for all she knew. There was so much else to worry about. Like what would happen after dinner.

The soup smelled delicious...but it had a faint hint of garlic. She set it aside.

The salad was good—but crunchy. Surely it didn't sound as loud to Rafe as it did to her as she chewed? Just in case it did, she only had a couple of bites of that, too. She speared a piece of asparagus, and tried to start a conversation, wanting to fill the silence. "I thought the meeting went really well—"

"I don't want to talk about business, Lauren."

"Oh." She ate another bite, trying to come up with a better topic. "I heard it snowed in the city today."

"That's nice."

Lauren stared at him, then looked down at her plate. Why was this so hard? she wondered as she took another bite of asparagus. This was supposed to be easy, fun, being together. But nothing seemed easy tonight.

She ate all her asparagus, three bites of steak—and passed on the potato.

Rafe put down his fork and frowned at her. "Aren't you hungry?"

She shook her head.

"Not even for the chocolate mousse?"

She shook her head again.

He stared at her a moment, and his eyes slowly darkened. He pushed back his chair.

Oh, oh, he's moving on to the next course, Lauren thought with a sudden flutter of panic, *which just happens to be me.*

He stood up and she tensed. She watched him as he began to turn off all the lights until only the candles, the fireplace and one lamp remained to light the room.

"What are you doing?" she asked, her voice squeaking a little as he reached for the last switch.

He paused. "I want to show you something."

She was sure that he did. She just wasn't sure she was ready to see it.

He switched off the lamp. The flames in the fireplace glowed and the candlelight flickered in the darkened room. He walked over to the window and held out his hand. "Come here."

Oh, God. He expected her to walk over to him. On legs that felt oddly weak.

Slowly, she stood up and walked toward him, placing her hand in his. His warm fingers closed around hers. He drew her closer, then put his arm across her shoulders, turning with her to face the window. "Look." He reached out and pulled the cord to open the curtain.

The blue velvet drew back slowly, revealing a scene from a Christmas card. Light from the hotel spilled out across the snowy grounds, revealing pines and bushes and bare maple trees frosted with the gently falling snow.

"It's beautiful, Rafe."

His arm tightened, and he bent to kiss her. And he tasted like the wine, but she liked it on his tongue. He kissed her deeply, tenderly, until Lauren felt as though she was in a dream, with the firelight dancing in the shadows, and the snow falling outside. And Rafe's arms, warm and strong around her.

"I knew you'd enjoy the view," he said huskily. His hands stroked slowly up her bare back, then down again, slipping beneath the material. Lauren trembled and burrowed closer to his body. He rubbed his cheek against her hair. "It's fantastic in the summer, too. And in the fall."

He kissed her again, capturing her mouth. But Lauren found herself unable to give in to the passion that had swept her away before. Her mind felt oddly detached from her body, his last comment lingering in her thoughts.

The seduction had been well thought out—the inn, the beautiful room. The candles, music, flowers and wine. Meticulous in every detail, just like one of his takeovers. But while all this was new and wonderful to her, he'd been here before. Possibly with many women.

She'd known that, of course. She'd realized she wasn't the first for him. But she suddenly realized how desperately she needed to know that she'd be the last.

She broke away from his kiss, turning her face into his shoulder. His lips brushed her temple. He toyed with the strap of her dress. "You look so beautiful tonight."

That word again, she thought. She swallowed, and whispered, "I don't need compliments, Rafe. I just need to know what you feel."

He slid the strap down, and bent to kiss her cool skin. "I want you, Lauren. I want to make love to you." He pulled her tightly against his hard body. "Come to bed with me."

A small pain bloomed in her chest, as if she'd taken a sudden blow to the heart. "I don't have my nightgown," she murmured. It was a silly thing to say, but she couldn't seem to concentrate.

She could feel his cheek move as he smiled against her hair. "You're not going to need it."

The pain in her chest lingered, spreading—until she had to move out of his arms. She stepped away from him, to stare out the window at the cold white snow falling on the trees.

He hesitated behind her, then moved nearer again. "What's the matter, Lauren? Don't you want this?" His strong arms came around her as he spoke, crossing beneath her breasts. "Don't you want me?"

He pulled her back against him. Her shoulders rested against his chest, and the evidence of his desire nestled intimately against her bottom.

For a long moment, she savored his heat, his closeness. The feeling of safety and completeness she felt while held so firmly against him. Yes, she wanted this—she wanted him—but *all* of him. Not just his body, not just this night, but his love. Because without love, there'd be no safety, no fulfillment in his arms.

"Yes, I want you," she admitted softly, and instantly his arms tightened, holding her even closer. He nuzzled her cheek.

She turned her head away, but lifted her hands to cover his. Holding onto him, she added, "But although I've changed these last few weeks—my hair, my clothes—I'm still the same inside, Rafe. I believe in love and I also believe that without it, sex is simply a temporary physical release. Not the emotional bonding it's meant to be."

She clutched his hands tighter, and her voice grew huskier. "I want my first time—my every time—to be with a man who loves me. I need love in order for all this to be...right."

Rafe stiffened. Lauren waited, but he remained quiet, his arms still locked around her. The silence drew out, speaking more clearly than any words he could say.

And after a while, she shut her eyes. Tears burned behind her lids. She'd been fooling herself. There was nothing for him *to* say.

She opened her eyes again, and drew a harsh shuddering breath. She moved out of his arms, letting the cold shiver through her. The pain inside her spread, consuming her heart.

"Laurie?"

She couldn't look at him for fear that she might cry. A

few weeks ago, she might have given in, been desperate enough to take what little he offered. But she'd learned a lot about herself lately. She was willing to forego a white wedding. She was even willing to temporarily set aside thoughts of marriage. But she wasn't willing to give up on love.

She hurt—every inch of her hurt—from the effort it took not to step back into his arms. Because of the lump in her throat her voice sounded strained as she said, "No, Rafe, I don't want this, after all. It's not enough for me."

He didn't love her.

So, still without looking at him, she walked out the door.

Chapter Fifteen

He wasn't enough for her.

For the next week, whenever the thought surfaced, Rafe grimly forced it down again. He tried to concentrate on more important things, like the final report on the Bartlett takeover. Spread sheets, proposals and budgets. He got ready for another trip—one for up north Lauren had scheduled long ago—but then canceled it, deciding his time would be better spent and his thoughts more fully occupied working up a cost projection on another merger. But on Friday, as he caught himself staring out his office window, wondering what she was doing, he finally admitted none of it was working.

He couldn't stop thinking about Lauren, stop trying to figure out how the night he'd planned so carefully could have gone so wrong.

He'd bought her expensive flowers, a rare wine. He'd plied her with delicious food—that she'd hardly eaten—in an effort to give her a night she'd never forget. They'd talked. They'd touched. They'd kissed.

And she'd run away.

He swiveled his chair to face his desk, the memory cutting through him all over again. Letting her walk out the door had torn him apart. He'd wanted to argue, to talk her out of her decision. To burn away her last-minute qualms with desire. But he'd let her leave and had paced his room for an hour, giving her time to change her mind, giving himself time to cool off. Then he'd gone to her room to try to straighten things out, only to discover she'd left.

Rafe's hand closed on a sheet of figures he'd compiled. He hated the way she had made him feel. Worried and tense with an emotion that had felt sickeningly like fear.

Still, he'd kept his cool, rationalizing that he'd smooth things over when he got home. He'd wrapped up the Bartlett project as quickly as possible the next day, and headed straight to her house.

He'd knocked and knocked at Lauren's door until finally Jay had opened hers. She'd told him that Lauren wasn't home, to leave her alone. That Lauren didn't want to see him anymore.

Pride prevented him from going back after that. No way was he going somewhere he wasn't wanted; he'd had enough of that as a kid. So he'd focused on the fact that he'd see her at work on Monday. He'd figured she'd have to talk to him then.

He'd lined up his defenses and arguments. Prepared his apologies and justifications. But she hadn't come in to hear them. Instead, all he'd gotten was a call from personnel, telling him Lauren was using her vacation time as her two weeks' notice. She'd quit over the phone—no excuses, no regrets.

Okay, fine, he'd thought. He got the message. He'd leave her alone. Except, thoughts of her wouldn't leave him alone. He'd find himself staring at her office as if she was still in there. As if she'd come through that door any second to give him one of her disapproving, scolding glances. One of her concerned looks. One of her smiles.

But she wouldn't. So he'd better get used to it.

He turned to stare out the window again. He didn't blame her for walking out, not really. He knew he wasn't the kind of man to fit her dreams. But if she'd been going to say no, then why the hell hadn't she done it sooner, instead of putting them both through agony? Because she'd wanted him, too, damn it. Just as much as he'd wanted her. Did she think he didn't know that? She might have fooled herself into believing she didn't, but she couldn't fool him. He'd seen the desire in her eyes. He'd felt the trembling of her lips. A few more minutes—a few more seconds—and she would have been his. At least for a little while.

If only he hadn't made that slipup, mentioning that he'd been in the hotel before. But that had been long, long ago. Before she'd even started working for him. He would have explained all that…except he hadn't wanted to get into his past too deeply.

He didn't want to remind her all over again that he wasn't the kind of man she wanted. She'd said it herself when she'd started on her quest. *Everyone isn't like you, Rafe. Only capable of brief affairs.* He'd wanted to argue with her evaluation, but he couldn't. They both knew he'd never had a "real" relationship. That he wasn't good "forever" material, a great candidate for marriage and family.

Hell, he hadn't even had a family since he was twelve. He'd learned to live with that. He'd had to, in order to survive being passed on from one foster home to another. And somehow, moving on—not getting too attached—had become a way of life. The marines had suited him perfectly—traveling from base to base, country to country.

College had been another temporary stop. Then he'd moved from firm to firm, fighting his way up the corporate ladder till he'd reached his present position at Kane Haley, Inc.

This was the place he'd stayed the longest, where he'd finally felt he could catch his breath. He'd even made a few friends here, like Kane. Most of all, this was the place where he'd found Lauren.

He'd known her three years—*three years!* There was no one else in his life he knew as well as he did her. Or cared about more. From the moment he'd met her, he'd liked her. They'd been good friends from the beginning. He'd never pushed for more, he'd never even thought of it—probably because he'd always known he wasn't right for her. But then she'd said a man was what she'd wanted, and everything had changed. After their kiss, he couldn't help wanting to be more than just her friend. To be her lover, an important part of her life, for a time.

But instead, he no longer had her in his life at all.

His hand tightened into a fist, and he realized he was still clutching the wad of paper. He threw it at the can. It bounced off the side and rolled on the carpet. Disgusted with himself, he shoved his chair back and stood up. He needed to get out of here awhile. To get some fresh air and clear his mind.

He left his office and went through hers, averting his eyes from her empty desk. He walked aimlessly down the hall, his hands shoved deep in his pockets. He got on the elevator—and got off again when it stopped to let on more passengers. He didn't want to talk; didn't want to have to be polite. He had no particular destination in mind, nowhere to go. He just wanted to keep moving to try to escape the feelings building inside.

He shouldn't be missing her so much, he thought, wandering down another hall. Women came and went in his life all the time, and he'd barely notice. He'd been alone since he was a kid, but he'd never—ever—been lonely.

But he was lonely without Lauren. He couldn't get her out of his head. Images of her kept plaguing him. The shock on her face when he'd asked her if she was pregnant. Her determined expression when she'd told him she wanted a man. The upside-down kiss she'd given him that night in her apartment. He kept picturing her face. Hearing her soft voice—

He stopped in his tracks, his mouth going dry. Was he going crazy? No, that *was* her voice. Coming from the cafeteria.

He glanced inside…and he saw her. With the instinctive reaction of a natural hunter, he drew back a little from the doorway, so he could watch her unseen.

She was standing high on a ladder, her slender arms lifted to attach a sprig of mistletoe to a wire hanging from the ceiling. She had on jeans and a green sweater. A red bandana covered her hair. She'd pushed her sleeves up on her forearms, the way she used to do whenever she'd try to make a basket.

Her expression was intent, a small crease furrowed her brow as she concentrated on what she was doing. Her mouth was pursed in a tense little bow. She looked pale and a little thinner, but wonderful.

Rafe was staring at her so hungrily, that it wasn't until Brandon, the kid from the mail room, spoke that he realized there were other people in the room—Brandon and old Artie Dodge.

"Hey, Lauren," Brandon called, from atop another ladder in a far corner. "Should I stick some mistletoe up here, too?"

"Let's not overdo it," Lauren told him, glancing in that direction. "I think garland is enough there."

Even from his vantage point, Rafe could read Brandon's expression. It plainly said, how could there possibly be too much mistletoe—or too many kisses? But when the boy spoke again, he asked another question. "Is the deejay you lined up supposed to be pretty good?"

"The best we could find."

"Does he play current stuff, d'ya know?"

Rafe watched Lauren's expression soften as she smiled at the kid. "He plays all kinds of music, Brandon. Something for everyone."

"Good." Artie's gruff voice sounded disgusted as he added, "Can't dance to the noise that passes for music these days at all."

Brandon had something to say about that, but Rafe didn't pay any attention as he looked around the room. Garland and tinsel were piled on a chair. Arrangements of poinsettias and candles were grouped on a table, next to a stack of red tablecloths. Obviously, Lauren and her crew were decorating the place for the Christmas party that evening.

He frowned. When Kane had learned Lauren had quit, he'd assigned Julia Parker to finish up the arrangements. But although he hadn't paid much attention at the time, Rafe had heard that Julia had been gone the past few days, out sick. She'd probably called up Lauren to double-check the arrangements, and, as usual, Lauren had responded by coming in to decorate.

The thought caused a soft ache in his heart. That was just like her. Lauren loved Christmas, and she wouldn't want anyone to be disappointed about the party. To most of the people he knew, Christmas was simply a time to put up decorations and get gifts. It meant drinking and celebrating and basically, an excuse to have a good time. It wasn't the trappings, but the spirit behind the holiday that was important to Lauren. She saw Christmas as an opportunity to give to people. To show them that she cared.

No, she wouldn't be able to leave this job undone, nor to refuse to help her friend Julia. Especially not when she was familiar enough with his own schedule to know that he was supposed to be out of town again. She'd probably thought there'd be no chance of running into him. Never-ever again—as she'd probably put it.

The thought hurt like a punch in the gut. His muscles tensed as he fought the urge to go over to her, to make her talk to him. He wanted to demand some answers. To make her listen to what he had to say. Hell, she was up on a ladder. No way could she escape him this time.

But of all the memories he had of her, the one that he kept thinking of the most was of the sadness in her eyes before she'd fled from the hotel room—fled from him.

So after one final, considering look at her, he walked away down the hall.

Lauren paused for a moment outside the cafeteria that evening. She peeked inside. Even to her critical gaze, the cafeteria's makeover appeared successful.

The round metal tables had been given elegance with the simple addition of red tablecloths and poinsettia centerpieces. The candles tucked in amongst the flowers gave the room a mellow glow, while the strings of twinkling white lights strung along the ceiling beams added a bit of sparkle to the shadowy room.

A colorful Christmas tree dominated one corner of the room, the makeshift bar another. The refreshment tables—laden with an assortment of dishes to satisfy every taste—

were lined up nearby. Along with the mouthwatering scents of turkey and ham, Lauren could smell cinnamon and apple from the huge bowl of wassail she'd placed on a corner of the table. The air was filled with the buzz of conversation and soft rock music.

Most of the people inside were laughing and talking in small groups. The newlyweds, Jack and Sharon Davies, were already moving around the space set aside as a dance floor. Ken Lawson was at the bar, and Matthew and Jennifer Holder were checking out the refreshment table. Everyone looked as if they were having a good time, as if they were happy to be there.

Except her.

Lauren glanced around again, but didn't see Rafe anywhere. Taking a deep breath, she made her way toward the refreshment tables to check the supplies. She hadn't wanted to come to the annual Kane Haley, Inc., Christmas party, but she hadn't been able to refuse. Not when Julia needed her help.

She'd tried to explain that to Jay earlier that evening, while getting ready for the party.

"Don't go back there," Jay had kept telling her as she'd styled Lauren's hair, curling and combing and talking nonstop. "You've already gone cold turkey on the man, quitting your job the way you did. I'm afraid that seeing him again will simply set back your recovery."

"He won't be there; he's off on a trip," Lauren had replied.

"Still, let someone else who works there help Julia."

"She asked me. Not very many people at the firm even know she's pregnant. She certainly doesn't want them to know that she's feeling sick. She just wants me to be there in case she needs to leave suddenly."

"And I don't want you to get hurt again," Jay had said softly.

Lauren's mouth turned down in a wry little grimace as she stared down at the food. She picked up a couple of the plates that were already empty and set them on a cart beneath the table. She couldn't blame Jay for being worried—she'd been pretty upset when Lauren had ended up at her door a week ago.

Walking out of Rafe's hotel room had been the hardest thing Lauren had ever done. Once back in her own room, she'd known she couldn't stay at the hotel with him so near, so she'd grabbed all the clothes that she'd packed with such care before and tossed them in her suitcase. She'd called a taxi and taken it all the way home. The cost had been well worth it. Every mile it put between her and Rafe was one more mile between herself and the temptation to run back into his arms again.

She hadn't cried during the long ride. But when she'd seen Jay and told her what had happened, grief for what might have been welled up in her heart along with her tears. Jay had comforted her with hugs and ice cream. She'd listened patiently, discussed every detail, until Lauren reached the conclusion—again and again—that there had been nothing else she could have done. Not once she knew Rafe didn't love her.

Yes, she'd done the right thing in leaving, Lauren thought, as she automatically rearranged the carrots on the vegetable platter. It was just too bad that doing the right thing was so painful.

Yet, painful or not, she needed to get on with her life. To put it all behind her.

"But what if Rafe shows up at the party?" Jay had asked her worriedly as she'd worked on her hair. "What will you do then?"

"I'll simply have to handle it. I can't keep hiding out from him forever," Lauren had replied quietly. "Running away was the only solution I could come up with at the time, but I don't want to make it a way of life."

Jay hadn't been convinced. "I still think going back there is like putting an alcoholic behind the bar to serve drinks at a wedding reception—the perfect setup for disaster. But if you insist on committing emotional suicide, you might as well go down in a blaze of beauty. I'll do your nails." She'd picked up a small bottle and shook it vigorously. "What color do you want? Crazy in Chicago Carmine? Or Insane Cinnamon?"

Lauren had chosen the cinnamon—not because she was insane, but because it matched her floor-length red formal, the one that left her shoulders bare. And she wasn't an alcoholic either. Her love for Rafe—her *previous* love for Rafe—she reminded herself sternly as she put out more meat pastries, was nothing but a state of mind that would alter with time and willpower and lots of affirmations. Not a disease.

Although she did feel a little sick with tension, she conceded, as, finished with her task, she glanced around the room again. She was just about to join Julia, whom she'd spotted standing all alone by the Christmas tree with her hands resting on the small mound of her stomach, when Lauren saw Rafe.

Her heart jumped and the knot in her stomach tightened. Nervous chills chased up and down her spine. He had a drink in one hand, the other was shoved into the pocket of his dark suit jacket. He was standing by Kane and Maggie. Maggie said something, and, as he tilted his head to listen, his crooked smile crossed his lean face.

Lauren's mouth went dry. She turned away, almost reeling toward the makeshift bar in the corner. She needed a drink.

But before she could get there, Brandon came up beside her. "Hey, Lauren. Thought you'd never get here." His bright, happy gaze skimmed her up and down. "Wow, you look hot."

"I do?" That was funny, Lauren thought, looking furtively over her shoulder to see what Rafe was doing now. Because the nervous chills had attacked her again, making her shiver.

"Yeah." Brandon's young voice was husky with admiration. "You look good in red."

Oh, he'd been talking about her dress, Lauren realized as she turned back to him. "Thank you, Brandon." She smoothed a hand over her skirt. "You look very nice, too."

He'd put on a sport coat for the occasion, along with a tie featuring the Grinch. A tide of red swept up his face at her compliment. "Do you wanna dance?" he blurted out.

Go out on the dance floor? Where Rafe might see her? No, she definitely didn't want to dance. But then she met Brandon's hopeful eyes and knew hiding out wasn't an option any longer. She squared her shoulders and smiled. "That would be nice, Brandon."

She fixed her eyes on a distant corner—the farthest away from Rafe—but Brandon steered her toward the center of the floor. The song was a fast one, a Latin tune with a heavy bass beat. Lauren tried to dance discreetly, keeping plenty of moving bodies between herself and the spot where she'd last seen Rafe. Brandon danced with abandon, his young, athletic body full of grace and vigor. He was undoubtedly the best dancer on the floor—the one to watch. Lauren tried to dance away a bit, to put more space between them. Brandon followed her like a pull-toy on a string, his hips thrusting energetically in a Ricky Martin imitation.

The song finally crashed to a halt. Lauren drew a deep sigh of relief. "Thank you, Brandon," she said breathlessly. "That was fun. I really—"

A light tap on her shoulder made her forget what she was going to say. Her breath caught and she turned around.

Artie was standing behind her. He beamed at her, his face wrinkling like a lovable hound's. "Would you like to dance, Miz Lauren?"

This time the music was a two-step. Lauren followed Artie's halting, arthritic steps sedately, one hand resting on his bent shoulder, the other held gently in his calloused palm.

They stumbled slightly and Artie's gnarled fingers tightened around hers. He concentrated, carefully regaining the beat before conversing again. When they were once more dancing steadily, he told her with a twinkle in his faded blue eyes, "Have to keep moving to stop all these young bucks from closing in. Part of the price of dancing with the prettiest girl in the room."

She wasn't the prettiest, of course. But the sincerity in Artie's voice bestowed beauty like a gift, and Lauren accepted it with a grateful smile. "Thank you, Artie. That is so sweet."

His narrow chest puffed out, the music drew to a close. And Lauren turned at another touch on her arm. This time Frank Stephens was standing there.

And so it went. Man after man, dance after dance. She circled the floor with James Griffin, with Ralph Riess and then with Brandon again. Even Kane Haley took a turn. Lauren had never been so popular, so sought after.

Somehow it didn't seem to matter much, possibly because she couldn't stop thinking about Rafe, watching for a glimpse of him. She was tense with apprehension at the thought of a confrontation, but he didn't come near her. Apparently he'd decided to leave her alone. That was a good thing—a wise thing—to do she realized, but still, a wave of sadness washed over her.

"It's a great party," Ken Lawson, her present dancing partner told her, breaking into her thoughts. "But there's one thing you've neglected...." He shook his head regretfully.

"What's that?" she asked, recognizing her cue.

"Mistletoe. Brandon was complaining about it to me, and I have to admit, the kid has a point."

Lauren smiled faintly. "From what I've heard around the water cooler, you don't rely on mistletoe as an excuse to kiss a woman, Ken."

"Hey!" He tried to look offended, but couldn't quite pull it off. "Let me tell you those nasty rumors are lies— every one of them. I'm an old-fashioned guy. I know the value of a great Christmas tradition."

He glanced up ahead a second, and Lauren realized he was steering her toward the mistletoe she'd hung in a corner of the room. Ken had already caught several women under the sprig. Apparently, she was destined to be his next victim.

But before he could maneuver her into place, they were interrupted.

"My turn," a deep voice said behind her.

Lauren's heart jumped into her throat. She glanced up at Rafe.

He met her eyes briefly, then looked at Ken, who appeared about to protest. But after a brief glance at Rafe, Ken gave in with a sigh. "Okay. Catch you later, Lauren."

"I wouldn't count on it," Rafe murmured as Ken turned

away, and the song drew to a close. Then he looked down at Lauren. "Hello," he said softly.

She swallowed to ease the tension in her throat. "Hi."

"Glad you came."

"So am I." There—she could do it. Make conversation with him without falling apart. Not scintillating conversation maybe, but still….

The music started up again. "Do you want to dance?"

Alarm rushed through her. "I, well, I—" She intended to say no, but before she could articulate a polite refusal Rafe had his arm around her waist and they were moving slowly across the floor.

Her hip burned where his palm rested. Her other hand tingled in his firm, warm grip. She knew she was trembling, but Rafe didn't seem to notice.

He said, "Your song, I think."

"My song?"

"'Lady in Red.'"

Until that second, Lauren hadn't even realized they were dancing to Chris Deburgh's slow, seductive love song.

"Yes, well, I'm definitely in red," she said, striving for a light tone.

"And you definitely look beautiful tonight." There was nothing light about Rafe's tone at all.

And suddenly, Lauren realized she shouldn't have come back, shouldn't have taken the chance of seeing him quite so soon. Jay had been right; she wasn't ready. Loving Rafe wasn't a state of mind that she could talk herself out of, she realized all over again, but the state of her heart, that would take time to heal.

She couldn't take it. She made a small, desperate bid for release, but this time Rafe didn't let her escape. He slowed to a stop.

"Lauren," he said huskily. "Look up."

Without thinking, she obeyed him. She saw the mistletoe, and then his eyes. She shut her own to escape his dark gaze and his mouth closed over hers.

Kissing him again was like heaven—and like hell. His lips were coaxing, persuasive. Possessive. It wasn't a long kiss, but it branded her deeply. And as soon as he lifted his head, she stepped away.

He was still holding her hand. She took a deep breath and lifted her chin. "I need to get back to work. To check the refreshments again."

But Rafe didn't seem to hear her. He turned and, still holding onto her, led her through the dancers and right out the door into the hall.

"Rafe—wait. Stop a minute."

He halted, then glanced around. He took a couple of steps toward a nearby door and opened it, tugging her inside after him. He pulled the door shut.

For a moment, darkness engulfed them. Then Rafe released her hand and hit a switch on the wall. The overhead light flickered on.

Lauren blinked and looked around in confusion. "Where are we?"

His gaze was fixed on her. He shrugged, not even bothering to glance around. "Kitchen supply closet, I think."

Huge cans of vegetables were stacked on the steel counters. Green beans, peaches—with the Jolly Green Giant smiling from the labels. There was an assortment of pots and pans as well. "So why," she asked, not quite meeting his eyes, "are we in the kitchen supply closet?"

"Because we need to talk."

"We've already talked, Rafe."

He shook his head. "You did—I didn't."

The reminder hurt. Her cheeks flushed with heat, then

paled again. She swallowed painfully. "Yes," she said quietly. "I know."

He reached for her. "Lauren—please—" He stepped toward her, but paused when she carefully backed away. His hands dropped.

The grim lines bracketing his mouth deepened. His eyes were serious as he said, "I'm sorry about that night. I never should have taken you to that hotel."

Something in his voice made Lauren's throat tighten. She didn't know what to say.

He met her gaze steadily. "I want us to start over. Make a new beginning."

"Rafe...." Her voice broke. She clasped her hands together. Why was he making this so hard? She looked at him miserably. "I need to go. I don't want to play this game anymore."

"This isn't a game." His shoulders tensed and he shifted restlessly. "It never has been with you."

Her disbelief must have been written on her face, because his jaw tightened. "I mean it. I know my record in the relationship department isn't good—hell, I've never been close enough to anyone to even call it a relationship. But you told me that you've changed on the outside, but not on the *inside*. Well, since I've met you, I've changed on the inside. I want more in my life than brief, meaningless affairs. I want to have someone in my corner, someone to build a life with."

His eyes grew darker, his tone more intense. He stepped closer. He was standing right in front of her now, and, before Lauren realized what he was doing, he caught her fingers in his. A slight shock ran through her at the feel of his warm skin.

He held her hand tighter. "This past week I've learned

just how terrible it is when you're not there. How much I miss you."

Pain filled his eyes. His husky voice grew softer but more urgent. "Please, sweetheart, come back to me. Without you I have no one to really talk to—no one to play with. There's no one to tease and watch out for."

He lifted her hand, cradling it against his cheek. Shutting his eyes he turned his face into her fingers, breathing the words against her palm. "Oh, Lauren. Without you, I have no one to love."

Love. The word hung in the air, then, like a raindrop in a pool, rippled through her. Spreading wonder, spreading joy.

Her eyes were wet, her smile bright as she stroked his lean cheek. "Oh, Rafe. I love you so much."

For a long moment, he just stared down at her without moving. Then he caught her in his arms, kissing her fiercely, thoroughly.

"Oh, Lauren. Sweetheart...." He kissed her again, then whispered against her mouth. "I want to be with you, every day and every night."

"Move in together, you mean?" she asked, tracing the determined line of his jaw.

"Damn right I want us to move in together—right after we get married." His arms tightened possessively. "I want you to belong to me completely—and I want every marauding male that ever comes near you to know it."

He reached into his pocket and Lauren's eyes widened as he pulled out a small black velvet box. He flipped open the lid, and removed the diamond solitaire inside.

"Oh, Rafe...." she choked out. Tears brightened her eyes as he slipped it on her finger.

She admired it, turning her hand this way and that,

watching it sparkle, as he took her in his arms again. "It's beautiful. It's gorgeous—"

"It says you're mine." And he sealed her mouth with a kiss.

Epilogue

One year later...

"**C**'mon, Rafe."

"No. It's Christmas Eve. We've had a nice dinner—a great dessert—and all I want to do now is relax."

Lauren let the silence stretch, broken only by the sound of the fire crackling in the hearth. Then she asked again in a cajoling tone. "Please? Just a quick one."

Rafe gave a long-suffering sigh and slouched down farther on the couch in the house they'd bought just outside the city. Turning his gaze away from the fire, he slanted a glance at his wife, who was sitting next to him. "They've all been quick lately. That's the problem."

"I'm sure you'll do better this time," she said primly.

"I would have done better the last time if you hadn't worn that damn nightgown to distract me," he replied with a low growl, feeling himself harden at the mere memory. He loved that white nightgown on Lauren. When he'd first seen her pacing slowly down the aisle behind Jay at their wedding, he'd thought she'd never looked lovelier than she did in her mother's white wedding dress. Then she'd come to bed on their honeymoon dressed in that silky nightie, and he'd changed his mind immediately.

He reached down to capture the slender fingers sliding stealthily along his side to the sensitive spot beneath his ribs, and glanced at her. His heart kicked up a beat, and his hand tightened around hers.

Fresh from her shower, she'd put on a pink sweat suit and her furry slippers to stay warm during dinner, and the outfit should have made a difference in the level of his desire. But it didn't help in the least. He knew how smooth her skin was beneath the cozy fleece. He'd explored with his hands and mouth every delicate hollow and womanly curve—and he planned to do so again very soon in their nice big bed.

He certainly didn't want to waste any time playing chess!

He opened his mouth to say so—then shut it again as he met her gaze. Her smoky-blue eyes had an expectant, hopeful expression and her soft lips were curved in a seductive smile. Damn it, she *knew* he was a sucker for that look.

He sighed, admitting defeat, and released her hand. "Fine. I'll play you. But just one game."

"Great!"

She jumped up to get the chess set while Rafe rose to pull a chair and small side table around in front of the couch. Lauren sat in the chair across from him, and immediately began setting out the pieces. They settled in to play.

In a ridiculously short time, Rafe realized he was in trouble. He was frowning over the board, sure she had

some devious plan in mind when she spoke again.
"Rafe?"

"Hmm?" He took hold of his knight.

"Let's make a bet."

He looked at her—something he'd been trying to avoid
doing because she'd been lightly rolling his pawn against
her lips ever since she'd captured it. An unfair, Freudian
distraction if he'd ever seen one.

He leaned back, narrowing his eyes at her. "What kind
of a bet?"

"Oh, I dunno. Just a friendly wager to make things in-
teresting." She waved his pawn in a vague gesture, then
tapped it against her lips again, pretending to think. "How
'bout if I win, we open presents this evening?"

He scowled. Damn it—he had *plans* for this evening!
Big plans that included Lauren lying naked in his arms in
front of the fire.

"And if you win, we open them in morning."

Rafe set his jaw. She looked way too confident for him
to agree to such a thing. "We agreed already to wait until
morning. I don't think—"

He broke off, his voice strangled in his throat as her
bare toes slipped under his pants leg. The little cheater had
kicked off her slippers under the table, and was obviously
intent on tormenting him. She stroked his calf then with-
drew her foot. Suddenly, he felt it again, gliding along his
inner thigh. Searching, no doubt, for the place that inter-
fered with his thinking.

Abruptly, he slid back, out of danger. "Fine," he
growled. "It's a bet." Grimly, he advanced his knight.

Two moves later, Lauren declared, "Checkmate." She
smiled at his stunned expression and rose, patting him on
the head as she sauntered past. "I'll get the presents. Mine
are in the bedroom."

Rafe stared at the board a moment longer, wondering where he'd gone wrong. Then, with a sigh, he put the pieces away. He'd obviously gone wrong when he'd taught Lauren to play chess.

He stood up and gave a huge stretch, then retrieved the present he'd bought her from beneath their tree which they'd decorated with twinkling lights, ornaments, and the little angel perched on top. He eyed the big pine consideringly. Opening their gifts shouldn't take too long. The scent of pine, the thought of the colored lights flickering on Lauren's bare skin was giving him a great idea....

Lauren came back into the room a few minutes later, wearing her "distracting" nightgown, and discovered Rafe sitting on the couch with a satisfied look on his face. Looking past him, she shook her head as she saw the pillow and blanket he'd cunningly placed beneath the tree. When it came to making love, the man didn't know the meaning of the word *enough*. Which was a very good thing for her.

She joined him on the couch, curling her legs beneath her.

"You first," Rafe said, handing her a small oblong package.

Lauren accepted it and carefully unwrapped the silver foil to reveal a black velvet jewel box. She lifted the lid, and gasped, tears springing to her eyes. "Oh, Rafe..."

He'd given her a diamond solitaire necklace, a perfect match for her engagement ring. She held it up, watching it sparkle in the firelight. "It's stunning. It's lovely. It's—why, it's Moustier."

"Yeah, well...." He pulled a wry face.

Lauren stifled a smile. "Can you help me put it on?"

She turned her back and Rafe deftly fastened the small hook. When she turned around again, he caught his breath. The diamond hung in the deep V of her nightgown, right between her breasts. "You look beautiful, sweetheart," he said huskily.

He went to take her in his arms, but Lauren gently held him off, saying, "Your turn." She handed him a large package.

"Hmm, what can this be?" Rafe said—as if he hadn't shaken the gift a hundred times since he'd found it in their closet. He ripped off the paper and a big smile crossed his face as he opened the box inside. Sure enough, just what he'd expected.

He lifted out the brown sweater she'd made him. "It's beautiful, sweetheart." He watched her face light up, then added, "But..." He hesitated.

"But what?" she demanded, taking the bait.

"But now that I don't have my yarn ball anymore, what am I going to play with?" He gave her a meaningful look.

She simply smiled, as she handed him another brightly wrapped gift. "This."

Rafe accepted the present curiously. This one had him puzzled. Shaking it hadn't revealed a thing.

And when he ripped the paper off, at first he thought the box inside was empty. All he could see were a few pieces of tissue. He glanced at her questioningly.

"Look again." Lauren's voice sounded oddly breathless.

He pawed through the tissue and discovered a couple strands of yarn, twisted together.

One pink. One blue.

His heart began pounding. His throat felt tight, but he forced out the words. "Are you—"

"Yes, I'm pregnant—we're pregnant!" she said, before he could complete the question. She threw herself into his arms, a glowing smile on his face.

"Oh, sweetheart...." His voice was choked. Rafe settled her across his lap and buried his face against her soft hair. "When?" he croaked huskily.

"Seven more months. Our baby should be here late in July." Never, Lauren thought, had she ever expected to see such a look of wonder on his face.

His dark eyes blazed, but the kiss he gave her was tender, sweet. Her arms were clinging around his neck when he lifted his head to look down at her again. "Oh, Laurie, I love you so much."

He hugged her, and Lauren rested her cheek against his heart. She smiled slightly as he dropped a kiss on her head, and spread his big hand protectively across her still-flat stomach. In a minute or so, she knew, he'd lie beside her on the nest he'd made beneath the tree, and they'd make love. Make another memory, another link in the chain of their life together.

She cherished those moments when he was inside her, as close to her as he could get. But she savored these moments, too. When, snug in his arms, she knew she was safe and warm.

And loved.

*   *   *   *   *

Turn the page for a sneak preview
of the next
HAVING THE BOSS'S BABY *title,*

LAST CHANCE FOR BABY

Raoul and Julia's story!
By favorite author Julianna Morris
on sale January 2002
in Silhouette Romance...

And don't miss any of the books in the
HAVING THE BOSS'S BABY *series,*
only from Silhouette Romance:

WHEN THE LIGHTS WENT OUT...,
October 2001
by Judy Christenberry

PREGNANT PROPOSAL, November 2001
by Elizabeth Harbison

THE MAKEOVER TAKEOVER,
December 2001
by Sandra Paul

LAST CHANCE FOR BABY, January 2002
by Julianna Morris

SHE'S HAVING MY BABY!, February 2002
by Raye Morgan

Chapter One

The phone on Julia's desk buzzed, and she gratefully pushed her lunch aside—milk and a package of crackers—and picked up the receiver. "Yes?"

"This is Trudy, in reception. I was told to notify you when Mr. Oman arrived."

"Thank you. I'll be right down."

"I'll tell him, Miss Parker." Trudy sounded starstruck, which wasn't surprising. One look at Sheik Raoul Oman and she must have melted in her chair. The man had sex appeal.

Julia glanced in a mirror and smoothed her fingers over a stray lock of hair. She didn't care if she looked attractive, just neat and professional. Then, squaring her shoulders, she went to the elevator and punched the Down button. A minute later she stepped out and saw the back of Raoul's dark head. Flutters hit her midsection even harder, and she gulped down another wave of nausea.

"Sheik Oman," she said, congratulating herself on the

cool, even tone of her voice. "Welcome to Kane Haley, Inc."

Raoul turned with cat-like grace, one eyebrow lifting. "As you know, *Ms.* Parker, I do not use my title in America."

She knew. She also knew that nothing could make Raoul anything other than what he was—a member of the royal family in his own country of Hasan.

"Mr. Haley is tied up in a meeting this afternoon. He asked me to show you around," she said.

Raoul inclined his head and smiled. "Kane has already explained this matter. I requested that you might take his place."

"Oh."

Any hope that he'd forgotten some of the more *intimate* aspects of their relationship vanished at the dark heat in his eyes. He remembered everything. And he seemed to be reminding her that she was the one who'd chosen to say goodbye.

"Kane was not aware that we were...acquainted," Raoul murmured. "I thought you might have mentioned me."

"Kane is the president of the company. We talk about business-related matters," Julia explained, more uncomfortable than ever. "Not about people I've met...at a business conference."

"Ah." The subtle humor lingering in the depths of his brown eyes made her wince, but there wasn't anything she could say in protest. Raoul could communicate more with his eyes than most people did verbally, and right now he was laughing at her attempts to pretend nothing had happened between them.

"Well," she said briskly. "Shall we start?"

"That would be excellent."

They stepped inside the empty elevator car, and no sooner had the doors closed, than Raoul pressed the Hold button.

"Bien-aimée," he said softly. "It has been a long while."

"Not so long. Just two or three months," she tossed off, as if she didn't have a clear idea how much time had passed.

"Over six months," he corrected. "June was a beautiful time in your nation's capital."

She kept her gaze glued to the Hold button he was depressing. "We'd better get going, or someone will think the elevator is broken."

"They will simply think the machine is slow."

"Raoul—"

"Julia," he mocked, using her same exasperated tone. "It is good to hear that you remember my first name."

Unaccustomed heat bloomed in her face. "I remember."

"As I do." He lifted his free hand and stroked the curve of her cheek. "I remember many things."

"Please, Raoul. It was nice, but it was just one of those temporary things."

"I did not choose for it to be so very temporary. You are the one who made this decision."

"We really have to be going," she said. She tried pulling his hand away from her face, but he held fast. "Raoul, let go."

"We must talk."

"We have nothing to talk about," Julia snapped.

"Julia…I still want you."

CALL THE ONES YOU LOVE OVER THE HOLIDAYS!

Save $25 off future book purchases when you buy any four Harlequin® or Silhouette® books in October, November and December 2001,

PLUS

receive a phone card good for 15 minutes of long-distance calls to anyone you want in North America!

WHAT AN INCREDIBLE DEAL!

Just fill out this form and attach 4 proofs of purchase (cash register receipts) from October, November and December 2001 books, and Harlequin Books will send you a coupon booklet worth a total savings of $25 off future purchases of Harlequin® and Silhouette® books, AND a 15-minute phone card to call the ones you love, anywhere in North America.

Please send this form, along with your cash register receipts as proofs of purchase, to:
In the USA: Harlequin Books, P.O. Box 9057, Buffalo, NY 14269-9057
In Canada: Harlequin Books, P.O. Box 622, Fort Erie, Ontario L2A 5X3
Cash register receipts must be dated no later than December 31, 2001.
Limit of 1 coupon booklet and phone card per household.
Please allow 4-6 weeks for delivery.

**I accept your offer! Enclosed are 4 proofs of purchase.
Please send me my coupon booklet
and a 15-minute phone card:**

Name: _____

Address: _____ City: _____

State/Prov.: _____ Zip/Postal Code: _____

Account Number (if available): _____

---

097 KJB DAGL
PHQ4013